"Why don[...] apartmen[...]

"After all," Lana continued, "you seem like a nice guy."

Greg wasn't a nice guy—everybody said so. But his neglected libido stirred. He could be a nice guy for an hour or so.

"That is, if *you* like *me*," she added shyly.

Greg couldn't believe it. While he was cooped up in his corner office, this kind of stuff was going on all over the city. Men and women were hooking up through singles ads for hot sex. Greg shook his head. No wonder life was passing him by. "What's not to like?"

Her smile lit up the room. "Great. Give me a sec to grab my coat and purse."

Greg's stomach churned with indecision as she walked away. She removed her apron, revealing a stunning silhouette. *Seeking single male for good time.* He'd never done anything like this in his life.

But when Lana turned her smile in his direction, Greg discarded rational thought. Why the hell not? He was going for it!

"Are you ready?" she asked, hooking her arm through his.

He couldn't believe his luck. "Oh, I'm ready all right. Ready *and* willing."

Dear Reader,

Can true love be found in the singles ads—even if you don't place one? When Lana Martina finds herself in dire need of a roommate, she advertises for a female or gay male to help her share the rent. So when Greg Healey shows up, she figures the gorgeous guy is off-limits to her gender. Only, Greg is responding to a singles ad for his brother... And when free-spirited Lana starts talking about going back to her apartment, he concludes she's...well, adventurous. How can these two love-starved loners *ever* get together?

I hope you enjoy this lighthearted holiday romance in which several characters from my previous books make cameo appearances. (How many will you recognize?)

Watch for my next title in *Midnight Fantasies*, the 2001 BLAZE anthology, available in June. Then look for *Two Sexy!*, a sequel to that short story in the new, longer BLAZE line also scheduled to debut in 2001. For a complete list of my titles, please visit my Web site, www.stephaniebond.com.

And don't forget to share the wonderful world of romance novels with a friend this festive season!

Happy Holidays,

Stephanie Bond

Books by Stephanie Bond

HARLEQUIN TEMPTATION
685—MANHUNTING IN MISSISSIPPI
718—CLUB CUPID
751—ABOUT LAST NIGHT...
769—IT TAKES A REBEL
787—TOO HOT TO SLEEP

SEEKING SINGLE MALE
Stephanie Bond

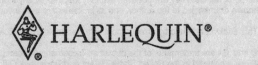

HARLEQUIN®

TORONTO • NEW YORK • LONDON
AMSTERDAM • PARIS • SYDNEY • HAMBURG
STOCKHOLM • ATHENS • TOKYO • MILAN • MADRID
PRAGUE • WARSAW • BUDAPEST • AUCKLAND

This book is dedicated to all the wonderful readers
who have taken the time to write letters to me about
the characters and stories that run around in my head.
Thank you, thank you, thank you.

ISBN 0-373-25905-0

SEEKING SINGLE MALE

1

Lexington, KY: SF in mid-twenties seeking SM for good times. Horse lover a plus. I'm a good cook. Coffee Girl

LEXINGTON ATTORNEY Greg Healey looked up from the ad circled in *Attitudes* magazine, his stomach twisting at the sight of his younger brother's wide smile. "You want to do *what?*"

"Meet Coffee Girl," Will said. "'SF' means single female, and 'SM' means single male—that's me."

Closing his eyes, Greg murmured, "Seeking single male."

"For good times," Will added eagerly. "Will you help me, Gregory?"

After a long morning of correcting real estate contracts, this he did *not* need. He sighed, then looked up into innocent brown eyes. Will's childlike expression seemed incongruous with his twenty-five-year-old body, which was broad and toned from grooming and riding horses at the farm that neighbored their home. Greg was tempted to dismiss his brother's request, but lately Will had been showing an elevated interest in women and dating. And in truth, considering Will's shyness and relative isolation, turning to the singles ads wasn't so far-fetched. The fact that his brother had ventured downtown to Greg's office to discuss the ad was proof that he was serious.

Still, intense protective feelings reared high. Greg gestured for his brother to sit in a plush visitor's chair, while he himself leaned against his desk and crossed his arms. "I don't think this is a good idea, buddy. You don't even know this woman—"

"But she likes horses and she likes to cook and she must like coffee." Will shrugged massive shoulders, as if he couldn't imagine what else mattered. "I love coffee, Gregory. Can I call her? There's a number at the bottom of the ad."

Greg bit down on his tongue, unable to offer an alternative for the handsome man before him who was obviously craving female companionship. The physical need, he could relate to, but Greg feared Will wouldn't be able to distinguish a physical attraction from an emotional one. And he was determined to shield Will from would-be opportunists with their sights set on his brother's half of the Healey family business.

"Will, women are...complicated creatures."

"Is that why you're not married, Gregory?"

Greg squirmed. Subtlety was not in Will's repertoire. "Er, yes." One of many reasons, the main one being he'd never met a woman who warranted the trouble of his becoming involved. Besides, most women seemed embarrassed by Will's presence, and his brother would always be his top priority.

Will scratched his temple. "But if women are complicated, then why do other men marry them?"

Greg gave him a wry grin. "Little brother, if you can answer that question, then you're a lot smarter than I am."

Will's eyes widened. "How about for sex?"

Okay, he'd asked for that one. Even after all this time, he still flew by the seat of his pants where Will was concerned. "You don't have to be married to have sex, Will."

"How often do *you* have sex, Gregory?"

He blinked. "That's a personal question." And pride barred him from answering truthfully. "Besides, how often one man has sex has nothing to do with how often another man has sex. Everyone is different. Do you understand?"

Will nodded. "Like how often you brush your teeth?"

"Er, something like that, yes."

Scooting to the edge of the chair, Will said, "I want to have sex, Gregory, but I want to be married first. Don't you think that's best?"

And how could he answer *that* question without being hypocritical? If he said yes and believed it, he would be sentencing himself to a life of celibacy, since marriage was nowhere in his plan. He inhaled deeply, then exhaled slowly. "Let's take it one step at a time, okay? First you need to meet a nice girl."

Excitement lit Will's entire face. "So I can call Coffee Girl?"

Greg massaged the bridge of his nose. His brother was a late bloomer with raging hormones. When mixed with Will's trusting nature, it was a recipe for trouble. The woman who placed the ad could be a hooker, for all they knew. On the other hand, a hooker would be preferable to a gold digger, or to a woman who would make fun of Will's mental disability. None of the scenarios that played out in his head had a good ending.

"Please, Gregory?"

This had to be what parenting felt like, Greg decided as he looked at his brother's hopeful expression. Being torn between good judgment and giving in. At last a compromise struck him. "How about if I check out this...Coffee Girl first?"

Will bit on his lower lip. "I don't know..."

"Will, don't I always take care of you?"

"Yes, Gregory." Will gestured toward the phone. "But will you call her right now?"

Greg hesitated, noting with alarm that his brother seemed fixated on the idea that this woman in the ad was somehow his soul mate. But the sooner Greg called, the sooner Will would realize that women were a disappointing lot.

"Sure, buddy, I'll call." Consulting the voice mailbox at the bottom of the ad, Greg dialed the number and, after the mechanical voice identified the mailbox, said, "Yes...I'm calling about your ad. My name is...Greg, and I'd like to meet you for...a cup of coffee." Feeling like a colossal fool, he left the number for his private office line and banged down the receiver.

"She wasn't home?" Will asked, his eyebrows knit.

"It doesn't work like that. The number is for a voice mailbox, where I left the message. The lady will call in to pick up the message, then she'll return my call. It's safer that way."

Will jumped to his feet. "But what if she doesn't call back?"

"She'll call."

"But what if she meets you for a cup of coffee and she likes *you*, Gregory?"

Greg draped his arm around his brother's shoulders. "You're the one looking for a woman, aren't you?"

"Yeah."

"And you're the horseman of the family, aren't you?"

"Yeah."

"Then don't worry."

Will frowned, obviously trying to follow the reasoning. "But when will *I* get to have coffee with her?"

"If she's a nice lady, then I'll introduce the two of you."

But not until she passed every test he planned to throw at the woman.

A grin transformed Will's face again. "Okay, Gregory." He gave Greg a giant bear hug. "Maybe we'll find a lady for you, too. One that's not so complicated."

With effort, Greg maintained a smile while Will waved goodbye, but as soon as his brother was out of sight, he leaned heavily on his desk. Gentle, big-hearted Will was always full of surprises, but this one had topped them all. Greg glanced at his desk piled high with papers, and heaved a sigh. *And now back to our tedious, mind-numbing program, already in progress.*

Moving in slow motion, he settled into his father's worn leather chair and tried to remember where he'd left off. Increasingly intricate real estate transactions had quadrupled the Healey Land Group's paperwork over the past year. At times he felt more like a pencil-pushing clerk than president and chief legal counsel. Rewriting mountains of contracts wasn't what he'd had in mind when he passed the bar exam a decade ago.

His phone bleeped, and he pushed a button with one hand while massaging a pain needling his temple with the other. "Yes, Peg?"

"I need your sign-off on plans for the company Christmas party on the twenty-second, sir."

He rolled his eyes. Was it his imagination, or had it only been six months since the last agonizing company Christmas party? "Are you within budget?"

"Yes, sir."

"Then go ahead with it."

"It's only two weeks away, and you haven't yet RSVPed, sir."

Greg sighed. "Will and I both are coming."

"Shall I put you down for two or four?"

Peg's polite way of asking if they were bringing dates, although they never had before. "Two, Peg. And I can't be interrupted right now." He knew he sounded like a grinch, but he couldn't help it—as far as he was concerned, Christmas simply heralded the end of another year of being trapped in this corner office. "Hold my calls."

"Yes, sir."

He stabbed the disconnect button, then walked to the window that consumed two entire walls of his office. The glass transferred the outside chill to his splayed hand, providing the most pleasurable experience of the prolonged morning. Downtown Lexington, Kentucky was all dressed up for the holidays with giant white plastic garlands and shiny blue bulbs twined around street lamps, the colors a tribute to the university.

Regardless of the season, his eyes were always drawn to the same building—the city courthouse. Indulging in a favorite daydream, he imagined how his life would be different if he'd gone into criminal law, instead of taking over the legal responsibilities for his father's real estate company when he'd graduated law school. Now, as the sole heir capable of running the business, he had no choice.

Greg reached up to loosen his tie in an attempt to assuage his sudden claustrophobia. Lately he'd had the pressing feeling that he was missing out on something, that life was passing him by. God, he hated the holidays. So damn lonely.

And now Will was wanting to leave him—or so it seemed.

Unable to face the paperwork that loomed large on his desk, Greg grabbed his gym bag and strode out the door. Without much success, he tried to push the singles ad business from his mind during his lunch-hour run, which he extended by a mile. For a reason that now escaped him, he'd never considered the day when his brother might marry and strike out on his own.

When their father had died seven years ago, Greg had sold his plush condo and moved back home, partly so Will could remain in familiar surroundings, partly to put the proceeds from his condo toward the mountain of debt their father had amassed. The bond the brothers had shared when they were children was forged even stronger, and Greg had simply assumed they would always live together, two happy bachelors.

Except, Will obviously wasn't completely happy. Later, as Greg toweled his neck, he admitted that some small part of him was grateful that his cynicism where women were concerned hadn't rubbed off on Will. But then again, it hadn't been an issue for a while; he hadn't dated anyone seriously since moving back home—the work required to get the family business headed back toward profitability had been enormous.

Oh, he'd had a few dinner dates here and there, but all the women had made their intentions rather clear—marriage. And their interest in his family's money had been equally apparent. He couldn't blame a woman for wanting financial security, but even a token interest in him, in his hobbies, in his dreams—was it too much to ask?

Of course, the real kicker was that, thanks to the string of bad investments their father had made before anyone realized his mind was slipping, the Healey brothers weren't worth nearly as much money as most people believed. He groaned as he stepped under the club shower, regretting more and more the call he'd made on Will's behalf. They had each other now—a woman would change everything, and not for the better.

When he returned to the office with a boxed lunch, he was cranky and favoring a pulled calf muscle. At the sight of a silver garland strung across his windows, he frowned. "Peg!"

The owlish woman appeared at his door. "Yes, sir?"

"I thought I said I didn't want my office decorated."

Her eyes bugged wider. "Do you want me to have it taken down, sir?"

He dragged a hand down his face and sighed. "No, never mind." He gestured to the slips of paper in her hand. "Do I have messages?"

"Yes, sir. Mr. Payton wants you to call him as soon as possible, sir. And a woman called about an ad, sir. Someone named...Coffee Girl?"

Heat flooded his face. "In the future, please don't answer my personal phone line."

"It rings so rarely—I thought it might be an emergency."

A nice way of saying he had no social life. "Did you say you took a message?"

"Yes, sir. Here it is, sir."

"Thank you," he chirped, then took the note and stuffed it into his pants pocket without looking at it. "That will be all."

Peg trotted out and closed the door.

Greg closed his eyes and counted to ten, willing away this restless, frustrated feeling that seemed to have escalated recently. He knew he needed to reduce the stress in his life, to simplify his obligations, but for the time being, things were what they were.

Glad for a reason to postpone contacting the woman from the singles ad, he phoned his general manager, Art Payton, convinced another problem was afoot. "Art, this is Greg. What's up?"

"Great news, Greg. The interest from developers is snowballing on the Hyde Parkland parcels." Art's hearty laugh rumbled over the line. "If the rezoning goes through, you could be sitting on the most valuable property in central Kentucky."

Greg refrained from reminding Art of his opposition to the acquisition of Regal Properties that Greg had targeted two years ago specifically *for* the Hyde Parkland property under its ownership. "Cut to the chase, Art. How valuable?"

"I'm talking about *serious* money. You could retire."

He managed a small laugh. "You're exaggerating." But he paced in front of the window to expend a burst of nervous energy.

"No, I'm not. If the rezoning goes through, you'll be set for life. Will, too, of course."

His feet stopped moving. Will was the sole reason he hadn't left the company when their father died. When he discovered the financial disaster they'd inherited, Greg had been thrust nearer to panic than he'd ever been in his life. He had to be certain that if something happened to him, Will would always be taken care of. If what Art was saying was true, the Hyde Parkland project would be the parachute he'd been hoping for.

"I'm telling you, Greg, this time next year you could be doing anything your heart desires."

Greg walked to the tinsel bedecked window, zeroed in on the courthouse roof, and smiled—actually smiled. Maybe this Christmas wouldn't be so bad, after all. Still, anything that sounded too good to be true... "I need more details, Art. Can we get together this afternoon?"

"How about three-thirty?"

"I'll see you then."

He slowly returned the handset, while hope thrashed in his chest. Was this deal the light at the end of a long tunnel? Greg shoved a fidgety hand into his pocket, and his fingers brushed the note Peg had given him. A groan welled in his chest, but a promise made to Will was a promise kept, so he pulled out the piece of paper.

Meet me at The Best Cuppa Joe tomorrow morning at eleven. Coffee Girl

Greg scowled and wadded the note into a ball. Romance—bah! As if he didn't have enough on his mind.

2

LANA MARTINA CONJURED UP a beaming smile for Miss Half-Caf-Nonfat-Whip-Extra-Mocha. Secretly Lana thought that without the fat, why bother with whipped cream at all. But then again, she didn't even drink coffee—an admitted peculiarity for the owner of a coffee shop—so she offered no comment. Especially since her customers were usually a bit testy before they had their first jolt of caffeine.

Ringing up the three hundred and fifty-sixth sale of the morning, she instead thanked her lucky stars for the large number of Lexington, Kentucky downtowners who relied on the ritual of sucking down coffee before facing their respective daily grinds. Addictions were profitable for the supplier, and Lana prided herself on supplying the best cup of Joe in the city. Ergo, the name of her shop: The Best Cuppa Joe. Okay, she couldn't take credit for the name since the shop had been located at 145 Hunt Street for thirty years—as long as she'd been alive—but she was proud to carry on the tradition as owner and manager for going on six months now.

The woman exited, and with the morning rush officially over, Lana slumped into the counter and willed away the anxiety roiling in her stomach. She'd promised herself she wouldn't turn into a workaholic entrepreneur, but lately one circumstance after another had made long hours unavoidable. Her pastry chef Annette had arrived at four-thirty a.m. with her regular supply of decadent muffins, bagels and baklava, but had sprained her ankle in the parking lot. Lana had sent her home, knowing she'd be shorthanded until Wesley clocked in before lunch.

Oh well, at least she'd be spared Annette's monologue about her ongoing manhunt. The girl was convinced her life was incomplete without the perfect man, and she never ran out of inventive ways to extend her search. Lana, on the other hand, had already found the perfect man. His name was Harry and his maintenance consisted of an occasional puff of air into the valve on the top of his rubber head. Harry never questioned her decisions, never wrestled for the remote, never criticized her hairstyle or clothing.

On the other hand, the only release Harry's anatomically correct body offered her was an occasional burst of laughter.

The bell on the door rang, and Lana straightened automatically until she recognized her friend Alexandria Stillman. "Oh, it's only you."

Alexandria glided toward the counter, sleek and catlike in a cobalt designer suit from her family's upscale department store across town. "Nice to see you, too."

Lana waved off Alex's comment and rubbed her aching pouring arm. "You know what I mean."

"Business is good, huh?"

Lana surveyed the space she'd come to love so fiercely, from the ancient brick walls to the whorled wood floors, to the slightly sagging stage where talented and not-so-talented hopefuls put their pride on the line during open-mike nights. A far cry from the claustro-phobic accounting office where she'd spent seven years of her life after college—holy humdrum.

"I can't complain," Lana said with a satisfied sigh, pouring a mug of the almond-flavored coffee Alex liked. "Do you have time to visit for a while?"

"That's why I came." Alex took the proffered cup.

Lana quirked an eyebrow. "Is Jack out of town?"

A blush stained Alex's cheeks. "Have I been neglecting you? I'm sorry."

"Since you've never looked better, *Mrs. Stillman*, I'll let you off the hook this time."

"Marriage does seem to agree with me," her friend gushed uncharacteristically. At least, the gushing had been uncharacteristic *before* she'd been swept off her feet by "Jack the Attack" Stillman.

"Yeah, yeah," Lana said with a grin. "Just don't turn into one of those marriage evangelists, okay?"

"I can't promise anything. Hey, do you have plans for Christmas Eve?"

A smile claimed her lips that for once, Alex didn't have to share her family for yet another holiday. "As a matter of fact, Janet is coming up."

"Great. I'm sure you and your mother will have a good time. If your plans change, though, you're welcome to come to Dad's."

Lana didn't respond. Maybe Janet had been a little unreliable in the past, but she'd come. She *would*.

Alex sipped the coffee and murmured her approval. "Nice hat, by the way."

Lana flicked the fuzzy ball at the end of the floppy red Santa hat. "Thanks. I wanted to go for the elf shoes, too, but my crew threatened to quit."

"Speaking of crew, where's Annette?"

"She sprained her ankle this morning, and I didn't want her to have to stand on it all day."

Alex tilted her head. "You look exhausted. Maybe you should sell yourself a cup of your energy blend."

"I'm not that desperate yet," Lana said, laughing. She pulled a bag of Earl Grey tea from beneath the counter and dropped it into a mug, then added steaming water from a dispenser. Janet, a bona fide Anglophile, had introduced her to tea as a youngster, and to tea she remained loyal.

"I guess I'm just stressed out over this roommate situation," Lana said. "I'm glad to be rid of Vile Vicki, but I can't afford to keep paying the entire rent much longer." Not and cover the lease on the coffee shop space, and the short-term note for new equipment, and the payments for the additional cash registers, refrigerator and pastry case.

"If you need a loan—"

Lana cut off her friend with a look. "I appreciate the offer, but no thanks." If she could squeak by for another year, she'd be able to pocket some of the profits instead of sinking all the money back into the business.

Alex relented with a nod. "Any responses from your roommate ads?"

They claimed a small square table painted with a red-and-black gameboard. Lana sat back in a padded chair and shook her head. "A couple dozen oddballs I wouldn't even consider."

"Oh, that's rich—you calling someone an oddball."

Lana pulled a face, then reached behind her to retrieve the magazine that lay discarded on a table. "I let Annette talk me into placing an ad, so maybe I'll hear something before Christmas, although it's a lousy time of the year to be looking for a roommate."

Alex leaned forward when Lana pointed out her ad:

Lexington, KY: SF seeking roommate, F or GM, non-smoker, preferably sane and willing to share kitchen duties.

"GM?" her friend asked.

"Gay male," Lana said matter-of-factly. "I don't want some straight guy getting the wrong idea about the sleeping arrangements."

"Oh, I don't know," Alex teased, tapping her finger on the singles ads on the next page. "Maybe you should've placed a combination ad and killed two birds with one stone."

"Oh, please. Don't start."

"You were the one hounding me to get a man before I met Jack."

"That was before I bought the coffee shop. Now I don't have time for scratch-off lottery tickets, much less a man."

"Are the ads national?"

"Yep."

"Well, you should be able to find a roommate over the entire country," Alex agreed, grinning over the brim of her cup.

Lana frowned. "Are you saying that I'm too picky?"

"Absolutely."

"Well, do you blame me, after living with that witch for so long?"

Alex blew onto the surface of her drink. "I'm just

wondering how much of the animosity for your former roommate had to do with the fact that she went out with the only man you ever cared about."

Ignoring the flash of pain that the memory of Bill Friar conjured up, Lana wagged her finger. "*Thought* I cared about. Bill Friar is a low-life cheat who was threatened by a woman smarter than he is." She'd trusted him, the cad. Lately she'd been pondering whether the problem was that she was too trusting of the people she cared about, or perversely drawn to untrustworthy people— excluding Alex, of course.

"Lana, you're smarter than anyone I know. Maybe you should start accepting invitations to those Mensa meetings to find a date."

"What? Holy hallucinogen, Alex, you know the only reason I maintain my membership in that uppity organization is for the insurance."

"Afraid of hooking up with a thinking man?"

She frowned at her friend. "No. I'd love to find a man with a big brain. But most eggheads are just that—eggheads. No life, no *passion.* Now, finding a man with a big brain *and* a big—"

The phone rang, cutting off her tirade, and spurring Alex's laughter. Lana sprang for the receiver. "Best Cuppa Joe, this is Lana. Merry Christmas, Happy Hanukkah, and a Cheery Kwanza."

"Lana, this is Marshall Ballou."

Of Ballou's Antique Clothing Boutique at the end of the block. "Hey, Marsh. What's up?"

"I just picked up my mail. Did you know there's a re-zoning meeting this Friday?"

Black dread ballooned in her stomach—so the rumor was true. "I hadn't heard yet, but of course I'll be there."

"I was hoping you'd say that, hon, because I was just talking to Vic and Paige and Maxie, and we'd like for you to be our spokeswoman."

She lifted her eyebrows. "Me?"

"What do you say?"

"I say you must be desperate."

"Quite the contrary, my dear, you're perfect. And we need you. The company that owns the property thinks they can railroad this rezoning plan through because it's our busy season and we won't notice."

Lana swallowed to force down the bad taste in her mouth. When she'd gone headfirst into debt to buy the coffee shop, she'd bought a virtual landmark. Everyone in Lexington knew there was a coffee shop at 145 Hunt Street. Parking was decent, the atmosphere was good. She'd never be able to build this kind of traffic at a new location—not enough to pay back her loans. "S-sure, Marsh, whatever I can do."

"Great. Call me after closing tonight. Gotta run."

Lana returned the receiver gingerly, telling herself not to panic. Yet.

"Bad news?" Alex asked.

"Potentially. There's a council meeting Friday night to introduce a rezoning plan for the blocks between here and Hyde. The local shop owners want me to be their mouthpiece."

"Good choice, since some of the council members already know who you are."

"Yeah, from *protest rallies*." She dropped into the chair. "I so do *not* need this right now. Besides, without the landlord's support, I don't believe it'll do much good."

"So get the landlord's support."

"We've tried, but the property is in the hands of so many holding companies, we haven't even been able to reach a real live person."

"I can have Daddy talk to his friend on the council and at least make them aware of the way the merchants have been ignored."

Her friend had offered help many times before—usually financial—but this was the first time Lana was desperate enough to take advantage of the clout the Tremont name commanded in the city. She touched Alex's hand and nodded. "Thanks. I know all of the shop owners will be grateful."

"Consider it done. If there's going to be a fight, at least it'll be a fair fight."

Lana puffed out her cheeks in a weary sigh. "So much for sleeping the rest of the week."

"Don't worry—you'll knock 'em dead." Alex stood and lifted her mug, but her obviously forced smile did not put Lana at ease. "I'd better get back to work. Thanks for the coffee." She walked to the door, then turned back with a little frown. "Cheery Kwanza?"

Lana shrugged.

Alex laughed. "Keep me posted on the roommate search."

Lana relinquished a smile as she watched the woman she'd known since junior high leave the shop with a sexy bounce to her step. Alex, it seemed, had nabbed the last gorgeous, independent, thinking man walking the face of the earth, or at least walking in the vicinity of the Bluegrass. Lana was happy for her friend, and sad for the rest of the female population, primarily herself. In times like these, it would have been nice to have a big, dependable shoulder to lean on. But since she'd bought the shop, she no longer had time to entertain her fantasies about a stranger arriving to sweep her off her feet. Now she'd settle for someone willing to sweep the floor.

With great effort, she pushed the upcoming council meeting from her mind while she tidied up the tables and plugged in the lights of the four Christmas trees on the stage. The liquid bubble lights on the smallest tree cheered her immensely. She loved this time of year—people were in a generous spirit during the holidays, if at no other time. It served a little glimpse into how things were supposed to be.

She worked around a college-age couple reading from a shared book and holding hands. A pang of envy cut through her chest. Young love was so sweet, so powerful. But she looked at the young woman and willed her to remain her own person, to follow her own interests, to make her own way. Not to marry out of sheer infatuation, then someday wake up dissatisfied with the life she'd built around another person's needs and wants.

Like her mother. The divorce had taken all of thirty days—and Lana hadn't even known until she'd dropped by her parents' apartment during a college class break and found her old room stacked with moving boxes. Janet now lived in Florida, selling tour packages and dating men that were wrong for her. Lana's father had bought a secondhand RV and hit the road with a chick named Mia. She hadn't seen him in years. The sordid clichés had broken Lana's heart. She'd thrown herself into her studies, determined to make something of herself that had nothing to do with a man.

About that time she had discovered The Best Cuppa Joe as a hangout. Old Mr. Haffner had given her grief about not liking coffee—but kept tea bags beneath the counter just for her. She loved the artsy feel of the place, the way musicians and poets and would-be philosophers gathered to try to solve the world's problems. Who would've thought that she would someday own the place?

She knocked over a mug and chastised herself for wasting precious time before the lunch rush. Picking up her pace, she carried table scraps to the back door and fed the two stray cats that magically appeared each morning. The day-old pastries went into a box to be delivered to a soup kitchen a few blocks away. Sorting the trash between serving customers took a while, with each recyclable going into its proper bin. When the morning chores were finished, Lana straightened the magazine she and Alex had been reading and decided to check the voice mailbox for the ad she'd placed. Juggling the receiver, she punched buttons while reaching for a pad of paper.

Eight calls—five men and three women. For one reason or another, none of them sounded exactly right. Then, remembering what Alex had said about her being too choosy, Lana replayed the messages and jotted down names, then just numbers when the pen threatened to run out of ink. Okay, so one of the women had a voice so annoying Lana struck her from the list, but she did return the rest of the calls, inviting the applicants to stop by the coffee shop for a chat as soon as possible— the first to make the grade would sign the lease.

She hung up the phone and turned to the mirror that ran along one wall to adjust her Santa hat. Her unruly pale hair stuck out from under it, hair that she'd finally whacked off in deference to the widow's peak and wavy texture. Her father had once said she was a hairbreadth from being albino, but instead of pinkish eyes, hers were violet. People thought she wore contact lenses, and when she told them different, they dubbed her eyes "spooky."

Funny thing, but when a person looked different, their behavior sometimes rose to the occasion. Even as a child, she'd stepped to the beat of a different drummer. Friends were hard to come by, doubly so since she was teased for living in a low-income apartment tenement. Teachers dismissed her as an oddity. A fluke pop quiz by a school administrator had led to IQ testing in the seventh grade. It was amazing how a "159" changed her in the eyes of her instructors. She was moved into private school on a scholarship, where she'd met Alexandria Tremont, heiress to a local department store chain. Their backgrounds couldn't have been more different, and their friendship couldn't have been more strong.

The warbling of the blue jay from the Birds of North America clock dragged her from her nostalgic musings. Ten o'clock—the lunch rush would start in an hour, and without Annette, it would be nuts. Thank goodness Wesley, a bespectacled college student, arrived a few minutes early.

But by eleven, customers were standing at the counter three-and four-deep. Lana deftly doled out coffee and bagels and biscotti until she was sure her arms would fall off. The rezoning meeting nagged at the back of her mind, although she tried to concentrate on each customer.

She glanced toward the door to gauge how long the rush would last, and did a double take when a seriously good-looking man walked in—tall, dark hair, wide features, great tie. On the heels of her initial assessment, disappointment set in. Such an interesting face for a working stiff. And holy houndstooth, hadn't she met enough shallow yuppie guys on her old job?

Yet she couldn't pull away her gaze, and to her surprise, the man stared back with such intensity that she wondered if she knew him from somewhere. He wasn't a regular customer, she was sure. In fact, he seemed more interested in her than in the menu. A second later, Lana laughed at herself—the man was probably there about the ad. When he claimed an empty booth without ordering, she was almost certain. It made perfect sense—all the best-looking specimens were gay. Although from the permanent wrinkle in his brow, this man appeared to be gay and depressed at the same time.

Oh well, if the man could cook and didn't steal, she'd be content. And just because he was gay didn't mean she couldn't enjoy the scenery. The crowd thinned in thirty minutes, and the man still loitered in the booth, occasionally glancing her way. Jeez, he might smile once in a while. When Wesley signaled he could handle the orders, Lana wiped her hands on her red apron and approached the man.

Upon closer inspection, the man was even better looking than she'd thought. His dark hair was closely shorn, his black eyebrows thick and expressive. His brown eyes were framed with heavy lashes and his skin glowed with health. Unusually affected, Lana overcompensated with a broad grin. "Hi! Would you happen to be here about the ad in *Attitudes*?"

He studied her for so long that she started to feel foolish. Then the man gave her a conservative smile and nodded his well-shaped head. "Yes. As a matter of fact, I am."

3

GREG STARED at the unusual-looking woman, tamping down his surprise. He had assumed that most women who placed singles ads were...desperate, shy or even homely. This woman appeared to be none of those things—the fuzzy Santa hat notwithstanding. In fact, her beauty slammed into him like a sucker punch. The white-blond hair that framed her perky face, and those violet-colored eyes—well, surely she was wearing contact lenses, but the color suited her enormously. His initial thought was that a woman this beautiful wouldn't be sincerely interested in Will, no matter how sweet his temperament.

A purely selfish reaction, he conceded a split second later. Because while he'd never denied his brother anything, he had to admit he wouldn't mind spending time with this woman himself.

"You must be Coffee Girl," he said stupidly, standing.

Her laugh was musical. "Well, my friends call me Lana. Lana Martina."

He luxuriated in her voice—smooth and full-bodied, like heavily creamed coffee. His vision tilted slightly, and he felt off balance. Suddenly remembering his manners, he extended his hand. "Greg Healey." Her handshake was firm and surprisingly strong.

"Nice to meet you, Greg. Would you like something to drink?"

"No, thank you." Only because his swallowing reflex was behaving strangely.

She gestured for him to sit, and they claimed opposite sides of the booth. Lana Martina was lean and long-limbed, and moved like a dancer. She also seemed completely at ease, so much so that he wondered how long she'd been placing singles ads. In his mind, he filled in the blanks: She worked a minimum-wage job at a coffee shop, and was hoping to snag a vulnerable, wealthy man. Like Will.

"Have you had a lot of responses to your ad?" he asked, at a loss for protocol.

"Several," she admitted, then smiled. "But you're the first person I've met face-to-face, so you'll have the best shot."

He blinked. First come, first served?

She looked around, then dipped her chin conspiratorially. "Look, this is a little awkward, but I have to ask—do you meet all the, um...requirements?"

"Requirements?" Those eyes of hers were mesmerizing, and so incredibly large. With a start he realized she was referring to the items in her ad—being a horse lover and someone who appreciates good cooking. Well, he wasn't a horseman like Will, but he could hold his own at the dinner table. "Uh, sure. And I make a pretty mean omelette myself." Had he *said* that?

She pursed her mouth as if impressed. "So, Greg, when were you looking to make a move?"

The woman was nothing if not to the point. Wiping his palms on his slacks, he said, "Well, I thought I might find out a little more about you first, like...where you live."

She laughed, nodding. "Sorry, I was getting a little ahead of myself. My apartment is on Wisteria, walking distance from here."

"I'm familiar with this area." He should be—he and Art

had discussed it in depth yesterday afternoon. In fact, the hazing of this building and the one next door were critical to their plans. Coffee Girl would be out of a job—but those were the breaks.

"Listen," she said. "I can step out for a moment. Why don't we go over to my apartment right now?"

Her words obliterated all real-estate-related thoughts. "Right now?"

She shrugged. "Sure. You seem like a nice guy."

He wasn't a nice guy—everyone said so. But his neglected sex stirred. He could be a nice guy for an hour or so.

"That is, if *you* like *me*," she added.

So...while he was cooped up in his corner office, this kind of stuff was going on all over the city. Men and women hooking up through singles ads for hot rendezvouses. Greg tingled with naiveté. No wonder he felt as if life were passing him by. He swallowed hard. "Wh-what's not to like?"

Her smile lit up the room. "Great. Give me a sec to grab my coat and purse."

The mention of her purse rang a bell. He needed to know if this was a *business* transaction. "Um, speaking of money..."

She dismissed his worry with a flip of her wrist. "If you like it, we'll talk about money later."

Greg's stomach and mind churned with indecision as she walked away. She removed her red apron, revealing a stunning silhouette. *Seeking single male for good times.* His collar felt moist. He ran his hand over his mouth. He'd never done anything remotely like this in his thirty-five years.

But when Lana turned her smile in his direction, Greg discarded rational thought. Why not? Why the hell not? He'd spent his life looking after his brother, his family's business—satisfying external obligations. Because he had no desire for a messy emotional relationship, his physical needs had gone unfulfilled. And here was Lady Luck, standing before him in a snug Christmas sweater. He was going for it, damn it. *Merry Christmas to me.*

She rejoined him, now hatless and pulling on a black-and-white spotted, fake fur coat more befitting of a ten-year-old. But he supposed most women with her, er, *hobby* were a tad on the flamboyant side.

"Are you ready?" she asked, hooking her arm through his in a familiar way that both startled and pleased him.

Greg's thoughts turned to the pocket in his wallet where he kept protection. If memory served, he had two condoms stashed there. Male satisfaction swelled in his chest. "I'm ready."

LANA SLID HER GAZE sideways at the handsome man walking next to her. The day was definitely looking up. The first person to respond to her ad seemed like a pretty cool guy, even if he was a little stiff. Greg Healey was certainly one of the most masculine gay men she'd ever met. She was a tall woman, and he was a full head taller. His profile was strong, his shoulders wide, his stride assertive. A bizarre thrill raced through her at his proximity, causing Lana to chastise herself. She wasn't the type of woman who would try to "convert" a gay man, but if she found out that he was intelligent on top of looking good, she was going to be supremely irritated.

Meanwhile, she liked him. There was something... undiscovered about him. In fact, she'd bet her tea bag that he was very recently out of the closet.

"So, Greg, what do you do for a living?" she asked, a few steps down the block.

"I'm an attorney," he said. From the tone of his voice, he

wasn't in love with his job. Little wonder, if he didn't make enough money to afford his own apartment. When he glanced at his watch, she said, "Don't worry—this shouldn't take long, so you can get right back to work."

He coughed, and Lana hoped he didn't have any kind of weird allergies, such as to rubber. Choosing between this guy and Harry, her blow-up doll, would be tough. "Any hobbies?"

"Hmm?" He looked as if she'd spoken in a foreign language.

"Hobbies?" she repeated with a laugh. "If we're going to be spending so much time together, I'd just like to know if you have any strange pastimes."

"I have a telescope," he said, then his cheeks reddened. "I mean, I used to enjoy astronomy."

Ah, a Science Club guy—how sweet. "Used to?"

"My job is rather demanding. I don't have a lot of free time."

"I can relate. What else should I know about you?"

He shrugged. "What do you want to know?"

Lana laughed. "Well, do you sleepwalk?"

At last he cracked a smile, an extraordinary smile that transformed his grave features. "No, I don't sleepwalk."

"Good, because I live on the third floor."

He suddenly looked uncertain, and his step slowed.

She winked. "You're not afraid of heights, are you?"

He ran his hand over his dark hair. The movement revealed the barest glints of silver. Suddenly he stopped, and a bemused expression came over his face. "Listen, um, Lana, this is pretty new to me."

Poor guy, he *was* still wrestling with coming out. "Don't worry," she said, laying a comforting hand on his arm. "I'll help you as much as I can. I want us to be friends, you know."

In fact, until this moment, she hadn't realized how much she missed having someone with whom she could share little things. Oh sure, Alex lived just down the hall—but Jack was there now, too, and they were building a home on Versailles Road, where the rich of Lexington migrated to live among endangered horse farms. She sensed an uncommon connection with Greg and hoped he would feel comfortable with her, too.

He shook his head. "But the money—"

"Hey, I'm fairly flexible. My rent is due on the first of the month, so as long as you pay me the day before, we're square."

He pursed his mouth. "Exactly how much money are we talking about?"

Ah—he was broke. A man who lived above his means, by the looks of his suit, and who probably hated the thought of having to share an apartment. Well, at least the man had good taste in clothing, even if he erred a bit on the Republican side. She smiled. "Four hundred a month."

He studied her, as if sizing up what kind of a roommate she'd make. "In return for?"

She gestured ahead of them to an ivy-covered brick structure. "There's my building up ahead. Why don't I just show you?"

More studying—Greg Healey was a studier. Suddenly, she very much wanted the chance to get to know him better. *Say yes*, she urged him silently.

His chest rose as he inhaled deeply, then he lifted his hands in a gesture of submission. "Okay, let's go."

GREG'S HEART POUNDED as he climbed the stairs behind Lana. He suspected, however, that his elevated pulse had more to do with the side-to-side motion of Lana's curvy behind than the exertion of ascending two flights of stairs.

"The elevator works most of the time," she offered over her shoulder. "But to be honest, it's so slow, I always take the stairs, anyway."

She talked as if he'd be spending a lot of time in the building, Greg noted. He had to admit he admired the woman's chutzpah. He followed her mutely through the door at the top of the stairs, into a corridor, then wound around two corners before stopping behind her in front of number thirty-six.

"This is it," she said, swinging open the wooden door.

As Greg stood rooted at the threshold, a tiny voice he recognized as his conscience whispered, *Don't do it. This woman is complicated.* Greg's nerve endings danced with indecision. He could still turn back. He *should* turn back.

But when she beamed a glorious smile his way, her eyes flashing an invitation, anticipation waxed over caution. A powerful surge of attraction hardened his sex. At this moment, he would have followed this beauty into a pit of tar. His feet must have moved, because suddenly he was standing in an eccentric, if slightly bare, loft. He barely took his eyes off Lana, whose sexual appeal now bordered on hazardous. His body strained for fulfillment. Greg wet his lips, feeling like a teenager in his haste to touch her.

"This is the living room," she said, practically bouncing on the heels of her thick-soled pink tennis shoes.

The "living room" was defined by a large red area rug in the shape of an apple. In contrast, the couch facing them was yellow; the chair, an oversize beanbag chair in University-of-Kentucky-blue. An enormous live Christmas tree stood against the wall, its branches bowed from the dozens of ornaments and dangling crystals. The scent of fresh evergreen stirred his senses even more. Sitting on a wooden stool was a small antique television sporting a rabbit-ear antenna contraption that extended into the air at least four feet.

"You're welcome to bring a bigger set if you want," she offered.

Did she plan on them watching that much TV? Scratching his head, Greg turned to the left and came up short, his heart skipping a beat at sight of the man standing mere inches in front of him. He felt foolish when he realized the "man" was a blow-up doll dressed in striped pajamas.

"Oh, meet Harry," Lana said with a grin. "He's my sidekick."

"Okay," Greg murmured. Even with the pajamas, it was clear that the doll was anatomically correct. A prop of Lana's?

She hung her coat on Harry's shoulder, then pivoted and swept an arm toward a galley-style kitchen decorated with...cows. Everywhere. Black-and-white, pink-nosed Jersey cows with fat udders. "Not much counter space," she said cheerfully. "But I'm willing to make room for your omelette pan."

Greg stared across the arm's length of space between them, and something...*unfamiliar* happened. Her gaze locked with his, and the static electricity in the air stung his skin. A weird humming noise sounded in his ears, like a frequency interrupted. God, she was lovely—her violet eyes, her pink mouth, her creamy skin. And with her leaning back against the gray-speckled counter, all he could think was how perfect the height would be for...good times.

She glanced away, and the moment was gone, perhaps a figment of his imagination to ease his guilt, a delusion that he shared some sort of connection with this stranger he was about to bed.

"And here—" she said, brushing by him to stand in a vacant area in front of two tall windows, "is where the table and chairs used to sit. I don't suppose you could fill up the space with something interesting?"

He swallowed at the picture she presented, her lush, willowy figure silhouetted by the midday sun slanting in through the windows, her hair a white halo. A piano. He'd buy her a baby grand piano if she'd only stand there a few moments longer.

Her eyes went wide. "Did you say a piano?"

Damn, had he spoken? A thermometer on his neck at this moment would have registered at least one hundred degrees Fahrenheit.

She clasped her hands together, her face lit up like a child's. "You're right, this would be the perfect spot for a piano! I haven't played in years, but it would be so fun!" Then her white teeth appeared on her lower lip, and she looked almost embarrassed. She grabbed both his hands in hers. "Greg, I don't mean to get all girly on you, but I just have a very good feeling about this situation."

He had the same feeling, and it made his pants tighter.

"I have this strange vibe that we were supposed to meet. Weird, huh?"

Her smile revealed a dimple in her chin. Greg might have thought it adorable, but he wasn't the kind of man who used the word *adorable*.

"Well—" she blushed "—I'm sure you'd like to see the bedroom."

If they didn't get down to it soon, he thought, limping slightly as he followed her, he might embarrass himself. On the far side of the loft, opposite the door they'd entered, a narrow hallway ran between two rooms partitioned off with permanent walls, but open to the vaulted ceiling. The bathroom is at the end of the hall," she said, pointing. "And this is the bedroom."

She pushed open the door to the room on the right and walked in a few steps ahead of him. He had the vague impression of a bed with white linens in the otherwise empty and modest room. The room where she…entertained?

Lana was talking, but he only caught a few words. "…great lighting…comfy mattress." Frankly, he couldn't concentrate on anything she was saying for watching her move. She was fine-boned, her arms long and lithe, her wrists small, her neck and collarbone well defined.

"So," she said, stopping in front of him and spreading her arms, "what do you think?"

Overcome with longing, Greg swallowed hard. The woman, his need, the circumstances—the combination overwhelmed him. His control was slipping, badly. "I think," he murmured, "that you are the most desirable woman I've ever met."

She stared at him and her lips parted. She blinked, but she couldn't hide the desire that flared in her eyes. Before he could change his mind, he reached up, curled his fingers around the back of her neck, and pulled her lips against his.

Their meeting was electric. Her mouth moved under his. Her sweet fragrance swirled in his nostrils, her tongue was as smooth as cream. She opened her lips, inviting him inside, where he foraged like a starved man. It was the perfect kiss, fueled by the tide of raw passion pulsing through his body. He'd never felt so in tune with a woman—they both wanted it. Wrapping his arms around her, he pulled her against him, reveling in the way her slim figure melded to him. His erection sought warm resistance, and found it against her thigh. He—

—was suddenly spun around and his arm yanked up between his shoulder blades. Greg grunted at the pain exploding in his rotator cuff. Before he could form a question, a knee in his back propelled him into the hall between the rooms. The wall stopped him. With his head smarting and his mind reeling, Greg straightened and turned around, but at the sight of the fuming blonde advancing on him, he backed into the living room. "Wh-what's wrong?"

"What's wrong?" she shouted. "What was that, that, that...*kiss* all about?"

"I thought you brought me here to..." He gestured helplessly toward the bedroom. "You know, for a good time."

Her eyes bugged. "*What?* How dare you!" She reached into the purse she'd set on the floor and withdrew a bottle of hair spray. "Get out before I call the police!"

Incredulous, Greg shook his head. "But your ad— *arrgghhh!*" He clawed at his eyes, which were suddenly filled with burning, clotting hair spray. "You're insane!" he gasped, blinded and feeling for the door. He found it, with the help of her foot on his backside. Greg tumbled through the opening and landed facedown on musty, smelly carpet. The door slammed shut behind him.

Greg lay there a few seconds before groaning and rolling to his back. Cursing under his breath, he rubbed his burning, watery eyes and tried to sort out what had just happened. The woman was obviously an unstable individual who set up men, teased them unmercifully, and then... what? Blackmailed them? Deciding he didn't want to wait to find out, Greg pushed himself to his feet, fished his handkerchief from his back pocket, and escaped the building while mopping his stricken eyes.

This was the reason he was single, and the reason Will would be better off as a bachelor, too. Women were like pet snakes—damn unpredictable. If he never saw the statuesque blonde again, it would be too soon.

4

LANA OPENED HER DOOR and peeked out into the empty hallway, hair spray poised. It looked as if Greg Healey—assuming that was his real name—was long gone, the baboon. He obviously hadn't expected her to object to his pilfered kiss.

And in truth, the kiss had been quite remarkable, but it was where the kiss was leading that she had a problem with. Lana pressed her fingers to her mouth, dizzy and a little perplexed as to why a guy who looked that good and kissed that well would resort to answering a lousy roommate ad on the remote chance of getting lucky. Strange. Very strange.

Heavy footsteps sounded in the opposite direction, and for a second she thought he'd come back, or had lost his way since his eyes were full of Aqua-Net. But instead, Jack Stillman loped around the corner, barefoot and wearing only jeans, his wet hair and torso evidence that he'd just stepped out of the shower. Holy he-man—Alex was one lucky woman.

"What's all the commotion?" he asked, his eyebrows drawn together. "Are you all right, Lana?"

She nodded, then waved in the direction of the exit. "Some guy answered my ad for a roommate, told me he was gay, and agreed to see the place." A wry frown pulled one side of her mouth back. "Then he tried to cop a feel in the bedroom."

Jack was trying not to smile. "Are you converting gay men now?"

"You're such a comedian, Jack."

"Seriously, did the guy hurt you?"

"No."

"Then what was that loud thump?"

"I threw him out, and he sort of, um, bounced off the wall."

He shook his head. "Alex assures me you can take care of yourself, but *why* would you invite a stranger to your apartment?"

"He looked trustworthy. And like I said, he said he was gay." Then she frowned. "Or rather, he let me *think* he was gay."

Jack scratched his temple. "Couldn't you tell?"

"What a completely homophobic thing to say."

He sighed. "Forget it. Should I go after the guy?"

Lana thought about it, then shook her head. "Nah. I don't think he's dangerous."

"You also thought he was gay."

"Yeah, but I don't think he meant to harm me. In fact, I had the strangest feeling he was...*scared* of me when I resisted."

"*I'm* scared of you," Jack said. "So, did you hurt him?"

"He has a few bruises, I suppose. And I sprayed him in the face with this—" She held up the pump spray bottle. "Extra hold."

Jack winced. "Do you know his name, just in case he shows up again?"

"He *said* his name was Greg Healey."

Her neighbor's eyes widened. "Greg Healey?"

She nodded. "He said he was an attorney. Do you know him?"

A laugh exploded from Jack's mouth. "I used to know *a* Greg Healey. But it can't be the same guy."

"Mid-thirties, dark hair, stuffed shirt."

Jack pursed his mouth. "Sounds right, but the Greg Healey I knew was a wealthy SOB—he wouldn't have been looking for a roommate. Damn unlikable. And for that matter, he wouldn't have been looking for a woman."

"Let me guess—he's gay?" she asked with an arched brow.

"No. But he was a seriously confirmed bachelor."

"Like you?" she teased, nodding toward the gleaming wedding band on his finger.

"More so," he assured her.

"Must be a different guy," she said with a shrug, wanting to erase the disturbing incident from her mind. "I guess I should chalk it up to experience and get back to the coffee shop."

Jack shook his finger. "Don't invite strange men back to your apartment until you know what you're dealing with."

She stood erect and saluted. "Sir, yes, sir." Lana pretended to click her tennis shoe heels together, then returned to her apartment for her purse and coat. But she was immensely troubled by the fact that equal to the relief for her safety, she felt a curious sense of loss. She had sensed a connection between herself and Greg Healey, darn it, and had been looking forward to a new friendship. Before he'd gone and ruined it all with that kiss of his.

Lana slipped her coat off Harry's shoulder, then angled her head at him. "I think we should make a pact, Harry old boy. If I haven't found a decent man by the time I'm ninety-five, and you still have air left in you, what say we tie the knot?"

He stared at her with a big permanent grin.

"Oh, good grief, don't tell me *you're* gay." She sighed,

tracing her finger around the lock of brown hair printed on his wide forehead. "I don't blame you—the man was rather extraordinary looking, wasn't he?"

Harry's big vacant eyes looked at her pityingly.

"I know, I'm getting desperate." She laughed ruefully. "It must be the holidays. Just don't tell anyone, okay?" Lana planted a kiss on his plastic cheek and walked out the door, trying to salvage her attitude. She wasn't about to give Greg Healey the satisfaction of ruining her day—not when so many other things were vying for that special honor.

GREG'S LINGERING INCREDULITY over his encounter with Lana Martina weighted his foot on the accelerator. The black Porsche coupe responded well to his frustration, gripping the curves of the winding driveway leading to the three-story house where he'd spent the majority of his life. His father had ordered that the sprawling structure on Versailles Road be constructed from genuine limestone mined from fertile Kentucky ground. The Healey homestead was a virtual fortress, and would be standing long after the family name died out.

And that would, quite possibly, happen fairly soon, since perpetuating the Healey name depended on his or Will's producing offspring. His parents had intended that the rooms be filled with grandchildren and great-grandchildren, but they hadn't counted on Greg's opposition to marriage, or on Will's special problems.

Flanked by towering hardwoods standing leafless but proud, the house never failed to lift his spirits. Until now. Now all he wanted was to take a shower, rinse his stinging eyes, and change his clothing that reeked of musty carpet.

The woman could certainly defend herself, he conceded. Almost as well as she could kiss. Not that it mattered, since she was a tease *and* a nut. He couldn't imagine how much that woman would have messed with Will's mind.

Spotting a large package by the front door, he parked in front of the four-car garage and made his way around the sweeping sidewalk to the main entrance. He caught a glimpse of his disheveled self in the glass of the doors and was glad their housekeeper, Yvonne, was away visiting her brother for a couple of days, or else she'd give him the third degree about his appearance and his impromptu trip home in the middle of the day.

But when he realized that the carton contained the saddle he'd ordered for Will for Christmas, he was almost glad for the incident; otherwise Will might have seen the box. *Almost* being the operative word, considering the bruises Coffee Girl had inflicted upon his person and his pride. Still, Greg admitted with a wry smile as he wrestled the box inside the door, it would be nice to surprise his brother for once.

"Whatcha got, Gregory?"

His brother's voice startled him so badly he nearly dropped the carton in the foyer. "Jesus, Will, I wasn't expecting you to be here."

Will held up a thick sandwich. "I forgot to pack my lunch this morning. Want some help?"

"No, that's okay—"

With his free arm, Will took the box from him as if it were a bale of goose down. "Is it a new telescope?"

Greg blinked. He hadn't thought of his broken telescope in months, and it had come up twice today, once with Miss Looney Tunes, and now with Will. "Er, yeah, it is," he lied, glad the return address label of Cloak's Saddlery had gone unnoticed.

"Good. I'll take it upstairs for you," Will said, hoisting

the box to his shoulder while nonchalantly taking a bite out of the sandwich.

Greg followed, shaking his head. He himself was a big man, but Will's stocky frame was solid muscle from his strenuous job on Kelty's stud farm that bordered their property. The gentle giant carried the carton to Greg's suite and deposited it in a closet, none the wiser that he'd just stowed his own gift.

Greg envied his brother sometimes—working outdoors, doing what he loved—and today was one of those times. Tugging on his tie, he suddenly dreaded returning to that damnable corner office. As far as he was concerned, the Hyde Parkland rezoning proposal couldn't be approved soon enough. He entertained a moment of vindictive pleasure at the knowledge that Lana Martina would be out of a job—she'd regret she hadn't earned that four hundred dollars when she'd had the chance.

"Gregory, your eye is bruised. Did someone hit you?" Will leaned close for a better look.

He sighed and ran a hand over his eye, wishing he could think of a good lie. But Will had to know how risky the singles scene could be. "I met Coffee Girl this morning."

His brother's eyes lit up. "You did?"

He hadn't told Will for this very reason—he hadn't wanted to give him false hope.

"Yes," Greg said, unbuttoning his sleeves. "She attacked me and sprayed hair spray in my eyes."

Will's head jutted forward. "Why?"

"Because she's—" At the wide-eyed innocence on his brother's face, he stopped and nodded toward a leather club chair. "Have a seat while I wash up, huh, buddy?"

"Okay."

Greg walked into the adjoining bathroom, stripped his shirt and flushed his eyes with handfuls of cool, soothing water. Sure enough, he'd gotten a shiner when he'd hit a wall—which wall, he wasn't sure. Pressing a towel against his tender eyelids, he nearly groaned in blessed relief. Meanwhile his mind raced as he tried to decide how many details about the encounter he should divulge to Will. Guilt churned in his stomach when he realized that his promise to help Will meet a girl had fled his mind as soon as he set eyes on Lana Martina. In hindsight, he'd gotten exactly what he deserved for being so pettily distracted from his goal.

"Are you okay, Gregory?"

He walked back into the bedroom, drying his face with the towel. "Yeah, I'm okay."

"So why did Coffee Girl attack you?" Will sat on the edge of his seat, wringing his big hands.

Greg dropped onto the side of his bed and slipped off his shoes. "Will, Coffee Girl isn't the woman for you."

His face fell. "Why not?"

"She's a..." *A lovely, bubbly, bright light whose medication wore off mid-kiss.* "She's a...um..." The only woman who'd ever managed to kick up his libido *and* kick his ass. He sighed, fidgeting.

His brother stood abruptly. "You told her I was s-slow, and she doesn't want to meet me."

Feeling morose, Greg stood and held out his hand. "No, Will, that's not it. In fact, I didn't even get to the point of mentioning your name."

He frowned. "Why not?"

"Trust me, buddy, this woman is...weird."

"Most people think *I'm* weird, Gregory."

Greg smiled. "No, I mean this lady is..." He floundered for words that would nip this whole singles ad business in the bud. "She's mentally unstable."

Will's expression was one of near fright. "Coffee Girl is crazy?"

"As a bat."

"That's too bad."

"Yeah, but I'm afraid that's the kind of desperate person who places those ads."

Will bit into his lip. "But I'm desperate, too."

"You're not desperate," Greg said, putting his arm around Will. "You're just impatient. Relax, okay?"

"Okay, Gregory. I know you'll help me find the right girl."

Greg pasted on a smile and bit his tongue to keep from saying such a girl didn't exist—for either one of them.

Will jerked his thumb toward the door. "I have to go back to the farm. They're bringing in Miner's Nephew today."

At last, something to really smile about. His brother loved his job, and the Keltys were good people to have given him the chance to prove himself.

"Can I look through your new telescope tonight, Gregory?"

He nodded, thinking now he had no choice but to buy a new telescope. And he gave quiet thanks that Will hadn't dwelled on Coffee Girl. After Will left, Greg showered quickly and changed into more casual clothes. He only wished *he* were able to dismiss Lana Martina so easily. The bizarre encounter plagued him as he jogged downstairs, and as he drove toward the science museum gift shop.

One minute she'd been enjoying the kiss as much as he, then she'd gone completely berserk. Maybe he'd simply been too assertive, or maybe—oh, hell, he'd probably never know what had caused the woman to snap.

Finally, the idea of buying a new telescope pushed troubling thoughts of Lana Martina from his mind. He called

Peg to let her know he'd be late returning from lunch. "Any messages?"

"Just two, sir. The closing on the Toler building has been moved to the twenty-third. And Art Payton called about the Friday rezoning meeting for the Hyde Parkland area. He can't attend because of a family emergency, and his key managers are committed elsewhere. Wanted you to know so you could send someone else, perhaps Ms. Hughs or Mr. Weber, sir?"

He hadn't been to a rezoning meeting in ages—usually they were routine and uncontested. But his future and Will's rested on the outcome of this particular meeting, so he wanted to ensure their interests were represented. Vigorously.

"Add the meeting to my schedule, Peg. I'll go." He hung up the phone and tried on a smile. Finally, something to look forward to.

---5---

"THE DOCTOR WHO WRAPPED my ankle was dreamy," Annette said as she slid the tray of cranberry Danishes into place. "But he was married, darn it, with four kids."

Lana rolled her eyes at yet another chapter in Annette's manhunt. The woman was a grown-up version of Little Orphan Annie, her petite figure overwhelmed by a helmet of wild red curls. Lana typically endured the woman's non-stop chatter good-naturedly, but her own usual good mood had been compromised by an unexplainable preoccupation with the man who'd called himself Greg Healey. All last evening she'd been restless, fidgety and irritated. Even a formidable amount of cake icing eaten straight from the carton hadn't helped.

Annette sighed dramatically. "I'll never get to wear my wedding gown."

Lana bit her tongue. Everyone who knew Annette had seen the wedding gown she'd been working on for going on ten years, because she carried it around in the back of her van on a mannequin.

"Mr. Right is out there somewhere, Lana, I just know it," Annette continued. "And he's looking for me, too."

"Well, if he's looking for you, I hope he likes coffee."

"From your mouth to God's ear. Hey, speaking of looking, have you found a roommate?"

Lana's laugh was as dry as yesterday's biscotti. "No, but I found a certified weirdo."

The pastry chef's eyes lit up curiously. "What happened?"

"A guy came in yesterday and said he was here about the ad. I asked him if he met all the requirements, meaning was he gay, and he said yes. He seemed all right, maybe a little stuffy, but definitely good-looking. But when I took him to see the apartment, he made a pass at me, right in the bedroom!"

Annette's face had gone totally white.

Lana laughed. "Oh, don't worry—I shot his eyes full of hair spray. But it was all very bizarre."

"Was his name Greg something-or-other?"

A tiny alarm went off in Lana's brain. "Do you *know* him?"

Annette touched a hand to her forehead. "Lana...oh my goodness, I completely forgot. A guy called about the singles ad I put in the paper, and I told him to meet me here yesterday at eleven a.m."

Lana's throat tightened—the timing was right. "You're running singles ads now?"

Annette nodded, her face red.

She gripped the counter. "What did your ad say, exactly?"

While Annette scrambled to find the magazine, Lana's mind swirled with the implication of a missed connection.

"Here it is," Annette said, smoothing the page on the counter. "'Lexington, Kentucky: Single female in mid-twenties seeking single male for good times. Horse lover a plus. I'm a good cook. Coffee Girl.'"

"Coffee Girl?" Lana murmured, remembering the man's puzzling enquiry.

"I thought it fit," Annette said with a sheepish shrug. "And I thought meeting in a public place was a good idea."

She had to sit down to sort through it all—while ignoring the tiny thrill that he'd mistaken her for someone in her mid-twenties. "You mean this guy I thought was answering my roommate ad was actually answering your singles ad?"

"I'm sorry, Lana. With going to the doctor and all, I forgot that I asked him to meet me here." She leaned in close. "But you said he was cute?"

Lana barely heard Annette as snatches of her conversation with Greg Healy came back to her and she realized how incriminating her words had been. She closed her eyes and managed a small hysterical laugh. He must have thought she was propositioning him. And being a red-blooded male, he'd accepted.

Then Lana froze as his other comments floated back to her. She swallowed a lump of mortification that lodged in her throat. Holy hooker! The man thought she was propositioning him, all right—for *money*.

"Lana," Annette said loudly, yanking her back to the present.

"Huh?"

The redhead's eyes glowed with hope. "You said he was cute?"

"I...guess so. But he made a pass at me, remember?"

"Well, you took him back to your apartment!"

"Yeah, but...if he were a decent guy, he wouldn't have gone!"

Annette's mouth was grim. "You're absolutely right. Any guy who would be that forward wouldn't be willing to wait until the wedding night, would he?"

Another one of Annette's romantic fantasies—that her gentleman prince would be willing to wait until their wedding night before consummating their relationship. Lana remembered Greg Healey's hot kiss, the split-second hardness of his sex against her thigh. "Er, no, he didn't strike me as the waiting type."

"Oh well, I'm just relieved that nothing bad happened. Thanks, Lana, for weeding out another loser."

Lana smirked. "That's me, the jerk strainer."

Annette grinned. "I'll bet he got more than he bargained for when he made that pass."

Lana returned a weak smile.

"Well, I'd better unload the rest of the doughnuts before the doors open."

When Annette exited to the back room, Lana rubbed her breastbone. Her internal organs had begun behaving strangely at the news that Greg Healey might not be the pervert she had originally thought. She swallowed hard, realizing that maybe Mr. Healey wasn't the only one who'd gotten more than he bargained for when he'd made that pass.

The alien sensation stayed with her throughout the day. Business was good due to a college sports conference going on downtown, and she found herself watching the door for the appearance of Greg Healey's tall, broad figure. It was silly, she knew, because the only reason the guy would come back would be to sue her for blinding him.

Her neighbor Jack's comments came back to her, and she idly wondered if this Greg Healey was the same rich SOB bachelor Jack used to know, after all. But if what Jack said was true, the Greg Healey he knew would be even less prone to answer a singles ad than an ad for a roommate.

She frowned. Unless the man simply shopped the singles ads for sex.

Her opinion of him continued to flip-flop. Lana even debated whether she should try to contact him and explain the misunderstanding. But she suspected he wouldn't find the situation quite so humorous.

No, better to let sleeping dogs lie. She'd lived in Lexington most of her adult life and had crossed paths with Greg Healey once. The chances of it happening again were astronomical.

Of course, when she arrived home that night, it occurred

to her that he knew where she lived. She would certainly feel better if she'd found a roommate, but she'd had no luck.

"You're too picky," Alex chided her when she came over that night to bring a velvet footstool she said she didn't want to haul to the new house. "And you should be careful about who you let in your apartment."

Lana sighed. "I suppose Jack told you what happened yesterday?"

"We have no secrets."

"Are you interested in hearing the rest of the story?"

Alex sat down on the yellow couch. "Absolutely."

Lana dropped onto the blue beanbag chair and watched as little foam balls went flying out of the tired seams. "The guy actually thought he was meeting someone who placed a singles ad."

Alex squinted. "Hmm?"

"My pastry chef, Annette, placed a singles ad and asked the guy to meet her at the coffee shop."

Her friend's eyes widened. "And he thought you were—"

"—looking for more than a roommate when I invited him up to see the apartment."

"Oh, that's hysterical."

"Oh, yeah, I'm still laughing about it," she said, rolling her eyes.

Alex tilted her head. "Wait a minute—why *aren't* you laughing? Did this guy scare you more than you're letting on?"

"Oh, no. He backed off as soon as I put up resistance."

"What is it, then?"

She laid her head back, wishing she could put her finger on this elusive unease. "It's nothing."

Alex gasped. "I don't believe it. You actually *liked* this guy, didn't you."

Lana lifted her head. "Are you insane?"

But her friend wore the most infuriatingly triumphant expression.

"That's it! You dig this Greg Healey." She clasped her hands together. "I'll have Jack call him up and—"

"Oh, no, you won't," Lana warned, shaking her finger. "I do not like this guy. I just…don't like the idea of him thinking I'm…loose."

"But he doesn't even know you."

"He knows my name and where I work and where I live. God only knows how many people he could tell."

Alex arched an eyebrow. "You practically beat him up. I'd say the man has as much incentive to keep it quiet as you do."

She frowned. "I guess you're right."

"Besides, if you're so worried about it, why don't you call him and set the record straight?" Alex suggested with a sly smile.

Lana frowned harder. "No, thanks."

"Okay," Alex said with a shrug. "If you change your mind—"

"I won't."

Alex relented with a nod, then gestured toward the ornament-laden evergreen. "I think it's leaning. Shall I warn the people in the apartment beneath you?"

Lana grinned, but her friend's awkward small talk alerted her to something more serious. "What's wrong, Alex? Wait a minute—you didn't come down to bring me a footstool, did you."

Sighing, her friend shook her head. "No. I came to show you this." From her jacket pocket she removed a folded sheet of paper and handed it to Lana.

Alex's father owned Tremont's, an upscale department store chain based in Lexington. Their downtown location occupied a city block, and they rented most of the first floor to eateries and service businesses. The space was expensive and in high demand, and overseeing the signing of the best mix of businesses was only part of Alex's job as the new president. The letter in Lana's hand was an enquiry about space from Buckhead Coffee. Dread flooded her chest. Buckhead was only the biggest, most commercial coffee chain in the country. The company had two locations in Louisville, but hadn't yet entered the Lexington market.

"We probably don't have the kind of space they're looking for," Alex said quickly.

"But they'll find it somewhere," Lana finished.

"But you already have lots of competition, and you're going strong."

Lana sighed. "But that's primarily due to my location, which is subject to change, depending on the outcome of the rezoning proposal before the council."

"Don't worry about this before you have to," Alex urged, standing. "I just wanted you to be forearmed."

Lana thanked her and walked her to the door. "This is good timing, at least. I have two days to come up with a brilliant speech for the council meeting."

"Do you know if the owner will be there?"

She nodded. "I called Regal Properties myself, and they guaranteed that a representative who had decision authority would be present. The shop owners are spoiling for a fight."

"I'll be there to cheer you on." Alex gave her a smile of encouragement. "But you might want to leave the hair spray at home."

Lana laughed. "I will. Besides, I daresay a lady-killer like Greg Healey won't be anywhere in the vicinity of a city council meeting on a Friday night."

6

"YOU'RE STILL WEARING your suit, Gregory. Do you have a date tonight?"

Greg smiled wryly over the dinner table. "A date with the city council."

Will's eyebrows came together. "The people who make decisions for the city?"

"That's right."

"Why do you have a date with them?"

"I want them to change the zoning for some property so we can sell it to developers who want to build homes."

"What's on the property now?"

"Some of the buildings are abandoned, some have small businesses in them."

His brother set down his fork. "What will happen to the small businesses?"

Greg saw where the conversation was headed. He glanced to their housekeeper Yvonne for help, but she gave him a look over the Parmesan chicken that said, "You're on your own, sonny."

He cleared his throat. "They'll relocate."

"You mean they'll have to move?"

"Yes."

"Do they want to move?"

Greg took a sip from his water glass. "Some of them probably don't want to move, no."

"Then I don't think you should make them."

"Will, we own the property. These people only rent space, like having an apartment. If you were renting an apartment, would you expect the owner to operate at a loss just so you wouldn't have to move?"

"No."

"This is the same principle. Besides, the business owners will have the opportunity to present their side to the council meeting tonight, too."

Will leaned forward. "Will there be girls at the council meeting, Gregory?"

Yvonne arched a gray eyebrow in Greg's direction. He shifted in his seat. "A few, I suppose."

"Maybe I could go with you."

"Er, you'd probably be bored, Will."

"I don't mind, Gregory."

He exchanged another glance with their housekeeper, then shrugged. "Sure, if you'd like to go."

Will's grin was so wide, Greg was sorry he hadn't suggested it himself. Will gestured to his own jeans and khaki shirt. "Should I wear a suit, too?"

The sweet innocence of Will wanting to impress a woman he hadn't even met pulled at Greg's heart. In his mind, there wasn't a female breathing who was good enough for Will. "No, buddy, you look just fine."

WET FROM THE DRIZZLING RAIN, Lana jogged into the community center where garland and paper snowflakes abounded, and glanced at the doors she passed, searching for the right room number. A minor emergency with the alarm system at the coffee shop had her running late. She had hoped to go home and change into something more impressive than hip-hugger jeans and a coffee-stained yellow smiley-face sweatshirt, but it couldn't be helped now. At last, she found the door to the room and slipped inside.

She was thankful the meeting hadn't yet started. Voices of what looked to be about one hundred people mingled in a low roar. Rows of folding chairs had been erected for participants, facing a long table at the front of the room where six council members sat talking among themselves. Margaret Wheeler—the president of the city council, if Lana's memory served—was giving an interview to a local news reporter. Lana's mouth went dry with nervousness.

From across the room, an arm waved. Marshall Ballou and some of the other merchants were sitting together. Alex was there, too, wearing a supportive smile. Lana made her way toward them, hoping they wouldn't be sorry they'd asked her to speak on their behalf. But she'd tried to do her homework, and her canvas tote was full of facts and figures.

"Are you nervous?" Marsh asked.

"A little."

"Just be yourself and let them know we're taking a stand."

In the front, the president pounded a gavel on a wooden block several times. "Everyone, please take your seats. If you're planning to speak on the issue of Rezoning Proposal 642, please sit near the front so you can access the standing microphone more easily."

Alex gave her arm a squeeze. "We'll be right here cheering you on."

Lana took a deep breath and moved through the settling crowd, searching for a seat. The gathering was much larger than she'd imagined. Her pulse kicked up at the thought that her life savings and livelihood could be swept away by a single decision from the six people sitting at the table, people who might remember her as a rabble-rouser on previous issues.

"You can sit here, ma'am," a man's kind voice said.

Lana turned and looked up at one of the largest men she'd ever seen. He was pleasingly handsome, and in command of a hulking muscular body. But there was something infinitely gentle in his eyes and his shy smile. He gestured to a seat in the second row that he had obviously just vacated.

"I don't want to take your seat," she protested.

"I'm glad to give up my seat for a lady," he said, enunciating very deliberately.

Lana suddenly realized the man had a slight mental deficiency or neurological disorder. She flashed him a grateful smile. "And I thought chivalry had died. Thank you very much."

The large man pointed to a black briefcase on the seat next to the one he was giving up. "My brother had to make a phone call, but he's coming back."

"I'll let him know how kind you were when he returns." Suddenly cheered by the stranger's thoughtfulness, Lana inhaled deeply and claimed the seat with an optimistic smile. Maybe this night wouldn't turn out so badly, after all.

"Excuse me." The kind man's brother had returned. She moved her knees sideways and shifted her bag in her lap to allow him to pass. The councilwoman banged again for the crowd to settle down. The man picked up his briefcase and dropped into the seat.

Lana turned her head. "Your brother gave me his—" She felt her jaw drop at the sight of Greg Healey. "You!"

His eyes flew wide, and he recoiled as if she'd hit him—again. "You!"

They vaulted to their feet and sprang away from each other, trampling toes of the people around them. Lana could not find her voice. A hot flush swept over her body. What the devil was *he* doing here?

"We need to get started," the woman in the front repeated loudly, and Lana realized that everyone was staring at them. "Please take your seats."

Lana eyed him warily, and he looked equally cautious. But when the silent stares around them became uncomfortable, they slowly reclaimed their seats. Lana sat rigid with shock. Every inch of her skin burned. Her mind spun with the coincidence of seeing him again and the inevitable embarrassment of explaining the mix-up. How would he react? Keenly distracted by his appearance and his proximity, Lana could barely concentrate on what was being said.

"...Margaret Wheeler, council president. Proceed to the microphone when your name is called. First, we'll hear from a representative from the city planner's office, who will read the proposal and define the specific area involved in the rezoning plan."

The lights were dimmed, plunging her into forced intimacy with the man next to her. The negative energy rolled off him in waves. An overhead projector kicked on, and a blurry map of the Hyde Parkland area appeared. A small man named Peterson droned on and on about the formal process of enacting a zoning change. She had contacted the city planner's office countless times to share her ideas about community conservation projects; Peterson thought she was a royal pest.

Suddenly Lana wanted to be anywhere but this blasted council meeting.

"Where is the man who was sitting there?" Greg Healey demanded close to her ear.

She jumped. "Your brother? I don't know," she whispered back. "He gave me his seat."

His soft snort could be translated to mean lots of things—none of them complimentary. She pulled away even farther, until she was practically in the lap of the woman sitting on the other side of her.

Lana faded in and out of the speaker's thirty-minute speech because she had already researched the tedious details he was providing. Instead, her mind zeroed in on Greg Healey, although she dared not look in his direction, not even with her peripheral vision. He was irritated, as evidenced by his frequent sighs and constant fidgeting. His chair creaked incessantly and the fabric of his suit slid back and forth, back and forth.

Her mind drifted as she recalled her first impression of him. Darkly handsome, friendly, even appealing. Holy hoodwink, looks could be *so* deceiving. Too late, she felt the heavy canvas bag slipping out of her lap. All twenty pounds of it hit the ground with a crash, punctuated nicely by Greg Healey's grunt of pain. She surmised his foot was underneath. Lana lunged forward to retrieve her bag, and promptly banged heads with him—hard. Pain exploded in her forehead. Their subsequent groans were audible enough to make people turn in their seats.

"Christ," he whispered hoarsely. "Are you some kind of lethal weapon?"

His breath was sweet, and just that easily she remembered how he'd tasted when he'd kissed her—like citrus and mint. "Keep your distance and you won't have to worry about it," she whispered back, ridiculously wondering if her own breath was as agreeable.

The lights came on suddenly, blinding her. The contents of her bag—binders, folders, papers of all kinds—lay all around their feet. She scraped the pages together, trying to return them to some semblance of order. At this rate, she was going to blow her entire presentation. He handed her a few items that had rolled out of reach, but he was wearing an inconvenienced frown.

"Why are you even here?" she asked, yanking the pages from his hands.

"Next on the agenda is Mr. Greg Healey," the councilwoman announced. Mr. Peterson had finished while they were arguing at knee level. "Mr. Healey will address us as the owner of Regal Properties, the company proposing the zone change."

He gave her a flat smile. "That's why I'm here."

Lana gaped. "You? You're...my *landlord?*"

"Landlord?" he asked, squinting.

"Following Mr. Healey, we'll hear from Ms. Lana Martina, who owns a coffee shop in Hyde Parkland. She'll be speaking on behalf of the business owners in the area."

She gave him a flat smile. "That's why *I'm* here."

He stared. "You *own* that coffee shop?"

"Gee, you're quick."

His frown was as black as Cuban coffee. "Then, yes, I'm your landlord. Do you mind letting me pass?"

Even under the artificial lighting she could see the fading bruises around his right eyebrow—bruises *she'd* inflicted. Numb, she straightened in her seat and shifted sideways so he could exit to the aisle. His pants leg brushed her knees, sending unreasonable tremors of awareness to her thighs. She caught Alex's wide-eyed gaze across the room. Her friend mouthed, *Is that the same guy?*

Lana nodded miserably. What had a few minutes ago seemed like an embarrassing encounter was now a bona fide disaster. She was going to have to debate the man she'd attacked? While he was still under the impression that she had taken him to her apartment to—

Holy Toledo, she was sunk.

7

GREG STEPPED UP to the microphone, forcing his mind away from the fact that the woman who had dominated his thoughts since their bizarre encounter a few days ago was not only sitting in this room, but planned to oppose him on the matter before the council. The coincidence was mind-boggling. He removed a folder from his briefcase with a hand that was somewhat less steady than he would have liked.

"Members of the City Council," he began, then turned to nod to the audience, "and concerned citizens." He scrupulously avoided looking in her direction, but he could feel those violet eyes boring into him. "The proposal before you would resurrect the once vital district of downtown known as the Hyde Parkland area." He directed that the lights be lowered, and recalled the sensation of sitting next to Lana Martina in the dark. The woman's tension practically glowed. Would she accuse him of trying to take advantage of her in front of everyone?

He cleared his throat and refocused. "This district is riddled with large, vacant buildings that once housed small factories. They've been vandalized and are beginning to pose a pest problem. None of the buildings, sewers or utilities are up to code, or suitable to attract the kinds of businesses necessary to revitalize the area." The words tumbled out more rapidly than he wanted, but he couldn't seem to slow down.

"Rezoning for residential development would mean hundreds of construction jobs for demolition and rebuilding. It would beautify the area, and attract home owners to Hyde Parkland. Property taxes would increase, as would business for the downtown merchants." Any second, he expected her to bolt from her seat and start shouting damning words.

"Is that all, Mr. Healey?" president Wheeler prompted.

"Er, no," he said, then inhaled deeply. Good grief, he had to keep his mind on the matter at hand. He fumbled with an acetate overlay for the map, upon which he drew black Xs over the buildings that were falling to ruin.

"My company has attempted to sell these properties for more than two years, but has found it impossible to interest business owners in making the investment that would be required for renovations. They can lease or buy ready-made real estate in the malls for less money, and so the dollars continue to be siphoned away from downtown Lexington."

He replaced the overlay with another one. "This drawing represents a restoration plan my company has worked out with the input of developers and the city planner's office. Single-family dwellings are in red, apartments in blue, condos in green."

"And the yellow?" president Wheeler asked.

The yellow area overlaid the buildings at 145 and 150 Hunt Street, where Lana Martina's shop was housed. He cleared his voice. "The yellow represents a parking garage."

He heard her gasp, even from across the room—and tensed for a blade in his back. "If the area were optimally developed, it could provide housing for more than twelve thousand people. And if we could increase the population within the city limits by a mere ten thousand, Lexington would qualify for an additional two million dollars in the form of government grants to upgrade utilities, to build more schools and to improve roads."

When the lights came up, the room remained quiet, which was a good sign.

"Once you read the detailed economic forecast for this rezoning proposal, I'm certain you'll see, the sooner the measure is approved, the sooner the city will begin to reap the benefits."

Wheeler nodded. "Thank you, Mr. Healey."

"Yea, Gregory," came Will's voice from the back, accompanied by his enthusiastic applause, to which a few people contributed.

Greg conjured up a smile and waved to Will without encouraging him. Leave it to his big-hearted brother to applaud regardless of the occasion. And leave it to his big-hearted brother to offer his seat to the very woman Greg least wanted to meet again.

"Next, we'll hear from Ms. Martina," the president said.

Greg swallowed hard and returned his presentation to his briefcase. He wasn't worried about what the woman might say regarding the rezoning project—hell, if her behavior ran true to form, she might *help* his case. But he had a feeling that he and Ms. Martina had at least one more confrontation in the cards.

When he turned and met her gaze, the feeling increased tenfold. Loathing emanated from those violet depths, reminding him yet again why he was single. With her chin lifted, she passed him, carrying the overloaded bag she'd dropped on his foot.

He returned to his seat, then pulled on his chin, waiting, wondering what the volatile woman might reveal. If he had to defend himself, what would he say? That he went back to her apartment thinking she wanted to have sex? That he thought a quickie with a beautiful stranger would lift him from the holiday doldrums?

Greg removed his handkerchief and mopped at the perspiration on his brow. Jesus, why hadn't he simply walked away?

"My name is Lana Martina," she said, her voice strong, her projection good. "I run a coffee shop in the proposed zoning area. In fact, I just discovered that I'm the parking garage."

The crowd tittered.

"I lease the building from Mr. Healey," she continued, then turned and gestured in his direction. "Although I didn't realize my landlord was an actual person until this evening."

The crowd laughed outright, and his face burned.

She turned back to the council members. "I'm speaking on behalf of thirteen Hyde Parkland shop owners. Part of the reason we're here tonight is that the ownership of the property is so deftly hidden in holding companies and leasing agents, we simply couldn't *find* the owner." She bestowed a magnanimous smile upon the council and the audience. "I'd like to believe that our being shuffled around like a deck of cards was simply an oversight, but I doubt it."

She knew how to work the crowd. A couple of the council members shot a disapproving glance in Greg's direction. He bit down on the inside of his cheek—he'd had no idea any of the shop owners had been misled or ignored.

Lana Martina plunked her own transparency on top of the rezoning map. "What Mr. Healey didn't tell you was that around the vacant buildings here, here, and here, are over a dozen viable businesses whose owners have a considerable investment in their locations and who will lose their livelihood if they're forced to move."

He frowned.

She whipped out another transparency, this one with statistics. "This graph shows that similar downtown rezoning projects in Dukeville and Franklin resulted in a *decrease* in city taxes because the residential buildings could not be filled and eventually were turned into low-income housing. The *reason* the residential buildings could not be filled to capacity was that the retail area, the character of the city, had been decimated, and there weren't enough attractions left to draw potential buyers downtown."

He blinked.

Forty minutes later, he'd lost count of the pie charts and bar graphs, not to mention handouts of the possible negative economical effects of his plan if 1) interest rates rose, 2) unemployment increased, or 3) property taxes jumped. She had projected housing costs, population growth and the effect on the city's declining sewer system, which was currently costing the city such-and-such in fines every day because untreated water was being dumped into a nearby lake.

"So as you can see," Lana said with a flourish, "the proposal before the council is far more than a simple rezoning project. You, ladies and gentlemen, might be held accountable for passing a proposal that would lead to the decline of the entire downtown economy simply to line the coffers of Regal Properties and—" she shot him a pointed look "—the pockets of Mr. Greg Healey."

The shop owners burst into applause, and Greg shifted in his chair. Despite the woman's emotional argument, however, he felt confident the city council would side with him. After all, leaving the zoning as is would only lead to more decline.

"Is that all, Ms. Martina?" the council president asked.

"Just one more thing," she said in a charming voice.

Greg's heartbeat thrashed in his ears. *She was going to spill her guts about their encounter.*

Leaning closer to the microphone, she said, "I'd like to go on record, saying that even the timing of the proposal is suspect, considering this is the busiest time of the year for those of us who run our own retail businesses." She sent a stinging look in his direction. "One might conclude the owner was trying to sneak this rezoning project by the shop owners and the city council."

A decidedly suspicious mood descended over the audience, and it was all directed toward Greg.

"Thank you for listening," she closed in a solemn tone typically reserved for eulogies.

Greg closed his eyes briefly, as the crowd once again erupted in applause. Christ, she was good. Everyone in the room either wanted to hire her or sleep with her. Except him, of course. And she'd as good as painted a bull's-eye on his back.

LANA GATHERED UP her papers, her heart beating a relieved tattoo that she'd gotten through the presentation. Actually, she felt an incredible rush of satisfaction, a sensation that lasted until she made eye contact with Greg Healey as she returned to her seat. The man's jaw was clenched, and his eyes were dark. Gone was the carefree Science Club guy she'd shot the breeze with on the way to her apartment. Here was the real Greg Healey, and he was the kind of person she loathed—powerful and greedy. She lowered herself into the chair, positioning herself on the edge farthest from him. The meeting couldn't end soon enough as far as she was concerned.

But there were more speakers: a few private citizens who wanted to voice their opinions, and two politicians who simply wanted to get their name and face in front of potential voters. At the end, the president called for a fifteen-minute recess so the members might confer. Lana's nerves jumped with the knowledge that her life as she knew it could be over in mere minutes. Oh sure, she might have six months to clear out. But the loans—holy Chapter 11, she'd have to return to the corporate world just to make a dent in her debts.

Before she could worry about what, if anything, to say to Greg Healey during the recess, Alex and her other friends gathered around, showering her with accolades while shooting barbed glances over her shoulder at the enemy. His energy prickled the skin on her back.

"I have to leave," Alex murmured, her eyes brimming with questions. "But call me tomorrow and tell me what the devil is going on."

"If I figure it out myself," she whispered back. As Alex slipped away, the council members filed back in, and the president banged for quiet.

"The members have considered the arguments presented this evening. A formal vote will take place the second week of January, but the council is not convinced that this proposal has been properly investigated. We will reconvene two days before the vote for final arguments on both sides. In the meantime, the council charges Mr. Healey and Ms. Martina to work together to come up with a compromise that will benefit both parties."

"But—" Lana said.

"But—" Greg said.

The banging gavel interrupted their protests. "Meeting adjourned."

8

LANA WAS STRUCK SPEECHLESS. Work with Greg Healey to
come up with a compromise? Her mind reeled with the
new development, her consolation being that he looked as
displeased as she, his handsome face caught somewhere
between bewilderment and mortification.

A week ago she hadn't known this man existed, yet in the
space of a few days their paths had intersected at rather bizarre crosshairs. She'd read about these kinds of coinci-
dences, something about the inevitability of two souls
crossing that were destined to meet from the beginning of
time. Her fingertips tingled. Did he feel it, this...*mystique*
that reverberated between them?

He leaned in close, and she held her breath.

"Did you set me up?" he demanded.

She gaped. "Excuse me?"

"I don't believe in coincidence."

So this was the real Greg Healey—condescending, arro-
gant. suspicious. Lana crossed her arms over her stained
sweatshirt. "Haven't you heard, Mr. Healey—it's a small,
small world. Or are you always this paranoid?"

The man's ears twitched.

She smirked. "Listen, about the other day—"

"Stop," he cut in, causing her to blink. "If you mention
what happened the other day to anyone, I'll slap a civil suit
on you for assault."

Maybe it was the fact that she knew he cooked a mean

omelette, or that she knew he liked astronomy, or that he'd told her she was the most desirable woman he'd ever met—but this man did not scare her. In fact, she realized she had this puffed-up Richie Rich right where she wanted him: off balance. A warm, fuzzy feeling of feminine power infused her chest.

"Oh, *please* sue me. Then I can tell the court how I had to defend myself with a bottle of hair spray from an unwelcome advance."

His expression was incredulous. "You invited me back to your apartment! You even talked about money, for heaven's sake."

"The only thing I charge for, Mr. Healey, is coffee."

"Really? Does 'four hundred a month' ring a bell?"

She shook her head and snorted softly. "Like I was *trying* to tell you earlier, there was a mix-up in the ads."

"Mix-up?"

"There were two ads, Mr. Healey, and I realized later that our wires got crossed. I thought you were answering my ad for a roommate."

He balked, and she actually enjoyed watching the color leave his face. "Room...mate?"

"Which was why I was giving you a tour of my apartment."

He shook his head. "I'm supposed to believe you were running *two* ads—one for a roommate and one for a...playmate?"

Lana hesitated. If she told him that her employee Annette had run the ad, would he arrange to meet Annette again? Annette didn't need this man trampling on the fairy-tale image of Mr. Right she had conjured up in her head. And despite Lana's warning, Annette might throw caution to the wind and agree to meet him, just because Lana had told her he was good-looking. And a smooth talker like Greg Healey might even talk Annette into giving up her fiercely guarded virginity, to no good end.

"Yes," she lied. "I ran two ads."

He looked dubious. "I think you made up this cockamamy story about two ads to save your pride."

Her laugh of outrage was genuine. "Deposit? Pay by the end of the month? If I *were* a prostitute, Mr. Healey, I'd be charging more than four hundred a month, and I *wouldn't* be offering term payments."

His ears moved again—*how did he do that?* She could tell he was starting to believe her. She almost felt sorry for him. Almost.

"But don't worry," she added, lowering her voice to a whisper. "I won't tell anyone that you shop the singles ads for sex."

His face turned a mottled crimson. "You—"

"Mr. Healey and Ms. Martina?"

She turned to see council president Wheeler walking toward them.

The older woman lifted an eyebrow. "I'm going to take the fact that the two of you are already talking as a good sign."

Greg cleared his throat and Lana extended a forced smile. Talking, yes, but the woman would probably faint if she knew what they'd been talking *about*.

"I'd like to check in with you both before we meet again, just to make sure everyone is working toward a resolution." The woman maintained a pleasant expression, but her eyes glittered a warning at Greg. Lana realized that president Wheeler was the friend of Alex's father who had been informed of the owner's lack of communication with the tenants. Not enough to sway the woman's vote, much less the entire council, but at least she was putting Greg Healey on notice.

"Of course," Greg said cordially, then removed a business card from an expensive-looking holder. As if as an afterthought, he extended one to Lana, as well.

She took it, her fingers carefully avoiding contact with his. His intense gaze skimmed over her, and she wished she could read his mind. Was he contrite? Shamed? Angry? Lana glanced away to rummage through her bag for her own business card and wound up dumping the contents on the floor before coming up with a handful. Greg Healey glanced at the neon-orange card cut in the shape of a coffee cup before he dropped it into his jacket pocket.

"Very original," president Wheeler said of the card. "And may I congratulate you on an impressive presentation, Ms. Martina."

"Thank you."

"I'm aware that you've taken a leadership role in many community issues, and I applaud your involvement. How do you feel about working directly with Mr. Healey on this matter?"

Caught off guard, Lana chanced a glance in his direction. His thick eyebrows came together and he shook his head ever so slightly.

"I—"

"Ms. Wheeler," Greg cut in with a disarming smile, "I've been thinking that my manager, Ms. Hughs, would be a more appropriate person to handle this project."

The woman shot Greg a stern look. "Mr. Healey, I think *you* are the appropriate person to handle this project. If that's agreeable to you, Ms. Martina?"

Lana pursed her lips and shrugged. "I'm nothing if not agreeable." She added a broad smile for emphasis.

A muscle ticked in his jaw. "In that case, I'm certain that Ms. Martina and I will be able to reach a *friendly* compromise for the good of the city."

Lana swallowed at the unfriendly way the man said "friendly."

"I'm betting on it," the president said, her tone bordering on parental. "Now if you'll excuse me..."

And the next thing Lana knew, she was alone with Greg and a big, fat, awkward silence.

"Well," she said, clasping her hands and rocking back on her heels.

"Well." The muscle in his jaw ticked again.

She sighed. "Look, what happened was pretty darn embarrassing for both of us, so why don't we just forget about it?"

Tic. "Fine with me."

The firm set of his mouth conjured up memories of the ill-fated kiss, pricking her senses. The roar of voices around them swelled, insulating them in a cocoon of awareness. In his black suit and ultraconservative tie, dark-headed, dark-eyed Greg Healey was quite possibly the best-looking man she'd ever seen. She wet her lips. Pity he had so many issues.

"Gregory?"

She turned to see the big man who'd given her his seat approaching. Her heart squeezed when she remembered he had clapped for his brother.

"Gregory, you were great."

And right before her eyes, Greg Healey transformed back into Science Club guy. "Thanks, pal."

"You were good, too," the brother said to Lana.

"Thank you." She extended her hand. "I'm Lana Martina."

He grinned. "I'm William Healey. But you can call me Will."

His good mood was like a breath of fresh air in the stifling atmosphere. "It's very nice to meet you, Will. Thank you again for giving up your seat. Are you interested in city politics?"

He shook his head. "I came because Gregory said there would be girls here."

She shot an amused expression toward "Gregory," who seemed less amused, but more tolerant of his brother than of...anyone else.

"Will, I'm sure Ms. Martina isn't interested in our *private* conversations."

"I'm riveted," she assured them with a little laugh, "but I really must get back to work. Good night, gentlemen."

"Do you need a ride?" Will offered.

She hadn't driven her moped because of the rain, and, in truth, she was dreading trying to find a taxi, but she wasn't about to test that look of warning on Greg Healey's face. "Thanks, anyway."

"But we have the big car," Will continued. "And plenty of room, don't we, Gregory?"

Greg poked his tongue into his cheek and nodded.

Suddenly gripped with a wicked urge to provoke the man, Lana brightened. "Well, since you have the *big* car..."

GREG WATCHED AS Will tucked Lana into the front passenger seat, holding an umbrella over her so she wouldn't melt. Greg slung water from the sleeves of his all-weather coat, then swung behind the wheel. His mind still reeled from her pronouncement that when she'd taken him back to her apartment, the only thing she'd been offering was a room to rent. Damn, she must think him a pervert. No wonder she'd gone on the attack.

Embarrassment coursed through him at their proximity. For such a slender woman, she seemed to fill up the roomy cab.

But in his own defense, damn it, she'd *heard* him call her

Coffee Girl—she should have known which one of her ads he'd been responding to. Jeez. Looking for love in one ad, and looking for a roommate in another. Complicated.

She sighed musically, as if he needed to be reminded that she was within arm's reach. He kept his gaze straight ahead, wondering what about this woman had made him forget himself that day to the point of considering *paying* her to sleep with him. Good God. On hindsight, the idea seemed so ludicrous, he should have known something was wrong. He'd never before allowed his lust for a woman to override his good sense.

For some reason Greg couldn't yet pinpoint, this woman was hazardous to his judgment, and right now all he wanted to do was put as much distance between himself and Lana Martina as possible. He'd sort things out at home. Alone. He latched on to the steering wheel with a grip meant to drain some of his frustration. His brother, on the other hand, was grinning like a fool as he closed the door and climbed into the back seat.

"This certainly is a big car," Lana said, surveying the interior of the four-door Mercedes.

"It was our dad's," Will said, leaning forward to stick his head between their seats. "He died seven years ago."

"I'm so sorry."

"Will," Greg chided as he turned over the engine. "I doubt that Ms. Martina wants the history of the Healey brothers." He'd never seen his brother so talkative around a stranger.

Her white teeth flashed in the dark. "Since we're going to be working together, why don't you call me 'Lana'?"

She smelled sweet, but then so did rat poison. "Okay," he murmured through gritted teeth. "*Lana.*"

"Since you own a coffee shop, Lana, you must like coffee, huh?" Will asked.

Concerned about the potential direction of the conversation, Greg cleared his throat noisily as he set the car in motion. "Will, why don't you sit back?" The last thing he needed was for his brother to find out she was Coffee Girl—his "intended."

But Lana's pleasing laugh filled the car. "Actually, Will, I have a confession to make."

Will's eyes bugged. "What is it?"

Greg pulled out into the traffic, mentally mapping the shortest route to The Best Cuppa Joe. "Will, sit back, please."

He did, for which Greg was thankful, although he remained riveted on their passenger. "What's your confession, Lana?"

"I don't like coffee."

"Really?"

Greg scoffed. "You're kidding."

"Nope. I drink tea."

"Don't you think it's a little hypocritical not to consume what you sell?"

"It's not just coffee that I sell," she protested. "I sell an experience—the aroma, the crowd, the gaming tables, the music. That's what my customers pay for when they buy a cup of coffee."

He tried not to frown, but the woman placed a tad too much importance on a product that was little more than a commodity you could buy at any fast-food drive-thru.

"Yvonne says Gregory drinks too much coffee," Will informed her.

"Yvonne?"

"She lives with us," his brother said happily.

"*Will,*" Greg admonished, shooting him a warning look. He felt Lana's gaze piercing him with questions. "Can we talk about something else?"

"Gregory bought a new telescope," Will said.

He rolled his eyes. His brother seemed determined to share the details of their life.

"Did he?" Lana asked. "Do you like to look at the stars, too, Will?"

He had to hand it to her, she didn't use the singsongy voice that most women used with Will, as if they were talking to a child.

"Oh, yeah. Gregory shows me how to connect the dots and come up with a picture in the sky."

"What kinds of pictures?" She actually sounded interested.

"The big water dipper, and the little one. And people, and animals. Maybe you can come to Gregory's bedroom sometime and see his telescope."

Greg closed his eyes briefly. "Will, allow someone else to talk, please."

"Thank you for the invitation, Will," Lana said, her voice breezy. "So the two of you live together?"

"And Yvonne," his brother reminded her.

"Of course," she said, nodding. "Where do you live?"

"On Versailles Road," Greg piped in before Will could answer and veer off on another tangent.

"I have a friend who's building a new home on Versailles Road. Alexandria Tremont?"

He sighed. She seemed bent on engaging him in conversation. "Is she associated with Tremont's department stores?"

"Her father founded the company, but Alex is the new president. And she recently married someone you might know—Jack Stillman?"

He frowned as the name tickled his memory. "Jack the Attack Stillman?"

"One and the same."

"I was a couple years ahead of him at UK."

"He remembered you, too. Let's see, how did he put it? That you were a 'seriously confirmed bachelor.'"

"What does that mean, Gregory?"

He swallowed and tightened his grip on the wheel. "It means, er..."

"It means that your brother wishes never to marry," Lana supplied.

If he didn't know better, he'd think she was laughing at him. And it sounded as though she must have told her friends about the "incident" and that was when Jack Stillman had remembered him. Were they laughing at him, too?

"Gregory thinks women are too complicated to marry."

"Really?" Lana asked.

"Here we are," Greg said in relief, pulling up in front of the coffee shop ablaze with Christmas lights. Even from the street he could see the place was alive with activity.

Will immediately bounded from the car into the rain to open her door, leaving Greg chagrined. Perhaps he'd forgotten how to behave around a woman. Did that explain why he'd jumped to the conclusion that Lana had wanted to—?

"I'm sorry," he blurted.

She glanced at him, her eyes wide in the lighted cab.

"For...what happened the other day," he said, speaking quickly. "I have no excuse for my behavior." A deprived libido didn't count.

Her smile cheered him ridiculously.

"I share some of the blame for the misunderstanding." she said. "We both were looking for...something else."

Her eyes were mesmerizing.

She straightened. "So, when can we get together to talk about business?"

He blinked. Business? Yes, business. "Why don't you call me," he said, more brusquely than he'd intended, "when you get your thoughts together."

"Sure," she murmured. "Thanks for the ride." She wet her lips, and he watched until the moisture disappeared. "I guess we'll be seeing a lot of each other over the next few weeks."

Rub it in, rub it in.

Suddenly she laughed. "Don't worry, I'll leave my hair spray holstered."

He bit down on his cheek. Was she going to throw salt on his wounded ego at every opportunity?

She slid one leg out the door, then turned back suddenly. "Oh, and one more thing."

He sighed. "What?"

"I really like your brother."

He watched her swing out, her curvy behind swaying as she stepped up onto the curb. He heard her laugh and guessed she'd said something clever to poor, unsuspecting Will, who walked with her to the door of the shop, holding the umbrella over her blond head. She smiled up at Will, and a foreign sensation bolted through Greg's chest. Jealousy? Impossible. He scoffed silently and focused on the swishing windshield wipers.

When Will slid into the passenger seat and banged the door closed, a grin split his face. "I like Lana. Don't you, Gregory?"

He pulled away, watching the rearview mirror until the lights of the coffee shop disappeared. "Er, well, I hardly know her."

"Are you going to ask her out on a date?"

He frowned. "Absolutely not. Lana Martina is not my type."

"Can I have her?"

Greg nearly swerved off the road. "What?"

"If you don't want to ask her out, can I have her, Gregory?"

"She's not a horse—you can't just 'claim' her. When it comes to dating, the woman sort of has to agree." He scratched his head. "What if...she already has a boyfriend?"

"She doesn't." Will grinned. "I asked her."

Well, of course he had. Greg tucked away the nugget of information, then shifted in his seat. "Will, sometimes women prefer it if you're a little aloof, not so assertive."

"What do you mean?"

His mind raced for a suitable answer. "I don't think you should rush into anything with Lana Martina. Trust me on this, okay, pal?"

"Okay," Will said happily. "Lana is worth waiting for."

Greg hunched down in his seat, miserable in his wet coat, wishing very much that he'd never heard the name Lana Martina.

9

"I CAN'T BELIEVE IT," Alex said. "I simply can't believe it's the same guy!"

"Believe it," Lana said, lifting her cup of tea.

"And now the two of you have to work together. Oh, this is *good*."

"Good? Alex, we'd just as soon set fire to each other."

"But you explained the mix-up, didn't you?"

She was still harboring the teensiest amount of guilt over allowing Greg to believe she had placed both ads. But it was for Annette's own good, after all. "Um, yeah."

"And?"

"Let's just say that things are still a little...strained."

"Well, no man likes to be turned down, no matter the circumstances."

Lana grunted her agreement. "Plus, I think it bothers him that I know he gets his kicks from the singles ads." A wicked smile curled her mouth. "Then it occurred to me that I might be able to use that little tidbit to my advantage."

Alex's eyes widened over her mug of coffee. "You're going to blackmail him?"

"No." Lana wagged her eyebrows. "But *he* doesn't know that."

Her friend laughed, then shook her head. "I don't know, it sounds dangerous."

"I'm not afraid of the man's law degree."

"That's not what I meant." Alex took a slow sip, then set down her cup. "I think there's something between you and Greg Healey."

Lana's mouth fell open. "What? You saw the man—Greg Healey is a poster boy for corporate greed."

"He's powerful, yes."

"Then there's that little sticking point about him leveling my coffee shop to build a parking garage. Alex, I can't stand him!"

Alex looked dubious. "There's a thin line between love and hate."

"But I'm indifferent!"

"People who are indifferent don't use exclamation points when they talk."

Lana rolled her eyes.

"And I find it curious that you failed to mention how handsome he is."

"Is he?" Lana asked, studying the way the milk swirled in her cup. "I hadn't noticed."

"Probably too many other things on your mind," Alex agreed solemnly, "which would account for those circles under your eyes."

She sipped from her cup carefully. "I stayed up late working on the ideas I want to discuss with Greg—I mean, with Mr. Healey." She didn't add that the reason she stayed up late was that the coincidental encounters with the aloof real estate guru had left her big-eyed and restless at two in the morning. She kept remembering the way they had walked arm-in-arm to her apartment. Their exchange had been casual and comfortable when she'd thought him harmless and of no threat to...what? Her livelihood? The little pocket of relationships she'd built around the coffee shop? Her self-imposed celibacy?

"Earth to Lana."

She blinked. "Hmm?"

"I said, did you come up with any good ideas?"

"Well, I'm no architect." She sighed and dragged the papers she'd been working on toward them. "But I tried to come up with different ways to combine commercial and residential dwellings."

They looked through the stack of plans, pencil drawings and scribbled notes.

Alex shook her head. "I'm sorry. I just don't see a painless solution."

"And I don't expect to find one," Lana admitted. "But I do hope that the pain can be borne by more than a small group of people."

"Greg Healey's shoulders looked like they could carry quite a load," Alex said with a sly smile.

Lana shook her pencil. "This is strictly a working relationship."

"It doesn't have to be."

She frowned even as the heat rose in her cheeks. "Alex, doesn't it strike you as a bit bizarre that a rich, good-looking bachelor has to resort to the personal ads?"

"Ah, so you *do* think he's good-looking."

"Don't change the subject."

"Maybe he's shy."

"Oh, yeah, he was a regular shrinking violet at the council meeting. The man's an ogre."

"Maybe he's shy with *women*."

"He made an unsolicited pass at me in my bedroom."

"Which means he finds you irresistible."

"Which means he thought I was easy."

Alex sighed. "Okay, you're right. If you think this guy's a jerk, then I believe you. Just remember, I thought Jack was a jerk when we first met."

"Jack *was* a jerk when you first met."

A seductive grin lit her friend's face. "A man can change."

Lana's shoulders drooped in exasperation. "Alex, if I had time for a man in my life, he wouldn't be Greg Healey, whose only redeeming quality seems to be his brother."

"Yeah, his brother sounds like a sweetheart. But Greg can't be all bad if he lives with his brother."

"And a woman named Yvonne."

"Oh. The plot thickens."

"Well, *something* is getting thicker, all right."

"When will you see the infamous Mr. Healey again?"

"I'm supposed to call him to set up a meeting as soon as I get my thoughts together." Lana tapped the pencil harder. Of course, no one had to know she was referring to her thoughts concerning Greg. She knew her plan to tease the man could backfire. But when a woman had her back to a wall, she did what she had to do with everything she had to do it with. For now, she'd let him stew.

"HAVE YOU TALKED to Lana, Gregory?"

"No." And if Will asked him one more time, he would surely have an aneurysm. "The meeting was only last night," he reminded him gently.

"I've been practicing how her name would sound. *Lana Healey.* Doesn't that sound great, Gregory?"

He cut into a sausage link with more energy than was required. "Beautiful, pal, just beautiful."

"Who is this Lana person?" Yvonne asked, glancing back and forth between them.

"Nobody," Greg said.

"A really pretty girl with white hair and purple eyes."

Yvonne lifted an eyebrow in Greg's direction.

He sighed. "She represented a group of business owners

in the council meeting last night," he said. "I'll be working with her to tweak a rezoning proposal. It's just a formality."

"Gregory wants to shut down her coffee shop," added Will.

Greg put down his fork and rubbed his scratchy eyes. "It's not that I want to shut down her business, Will. But *we* own the property, and it'll be worth a lot of money once the rezoning goes through."

"You sound confident that the proposal will be approved," Yvonne said.

"I believe it will, but thanks to Lana Martina, it'll be at least another month before we can get things moving."

"Ah, she's a rabble-rouser," Yvonne said with a hint of admiration. "Well, not much would have happened over the holidays, anyway."

"Whose side are you on?" he asked with a frown.

But he couldn't ruffle the woman who was more like a family member than an employee. "Yours, *grouch*, but Ms. Martina sounds like a person fighting for what she believes in."

"I want to marry her," Will announced.

Greg closed his eyes.

"Really?" Yvonne asked mildly.

"She has a nice smile."

"I see."

"Gregory, can I call Lana and ask her out on a date?"

Greg wiped his mouth. "I don't think that's a good idea."

"Why not?"

Greg tossed his napkin on his plate. *"Because, I just don't."*

Will pulled back, his expression wounded.

Remorse pushed the air out of his lungs in a noisy exhale. "I'm sorry, pal. I didn't mean to yell. I've got a lot on my mind right now."

"Will," Yvonne said quietly, "would you mind refilling the juice pitcher?"

His brother nodded, picking up the empty pitcher and exiting through the swinging door to the kitchen.

"Would you like to talk about it?" Yvonne asked.

"What?"

Her laugh was soft, abbreviated. "Greg, you've been in a disagreeable mood for fifteen years—and not without good reason. But when you snap at Will, I know something's wrong."

He sighed. "It's this obsession he has with finding a girlfriend."

"Seems perfectly natural to me."

"But he'll get hurt."

"Maybe. But that's between him and the woman, isn't it?"

"Will's welfare is *my* business."

She gave him a pointed look. "And one of these days, you might not be around. Don't you think Will deserves to build a life with someone?"

Gripped with a mounting frustration he couldn't identify, he silently chewed on the inside of his cheek.

"And while we're on the subject, Greg, you deserve the same."

He looked away. "I like my own company."

"And if you'd salvage what's left of your personality, someone else might like your company, too."

"This isn't about me."

"Isn't it?" she pressed.

He looked back to the middle-aged woman. "No. And I'm not going to stand by and watch Will have his hopes dashed by someone like Lana Martina."

"How do you know she'll dash his hopes?"

"Because she's—" he shot a glance toward the kitchen and lowered his voice "—out of his league."

"Oh. And would she happen to be in *your* league?"

He scowled. "What's that supposed to mean?"

She gave him a smile that only a woman who had bounced the brothers on her knee could get away with. He ground his teeth.

Will burst back into the room. "We were out of juice, so I brought milk. Want some, Gregory?"

Greg looked up at his brother's happy face and lifted his empty glass. "Sure."

"Gregory, I think I know why you don't want me to ask Lana Martina out on a date."

He choked on the milk he'd just swallowed. "Why?"

"Because she's against you on the rezoning proposal, and I should be on your side. I'm sorry, Gregory."

One hurt expression from Will was like a thousand knives in the heart. "You don't have to apologize, buddy. We're square, okay?"

"Okay." Will poured himself a huge glass of milk. "But I was thinking—if you have to win Lana Martina over to your side, shouldn't you try to be nice to her, Gregory?"

Flustered at Will's simple but unerring logic, he glanced to Yvonne, who lifted her glass of milk to silently second the suggestion.

Faced with two people with whom arguing was nearly impossible, Greg counted to ten silently, then resumed eating. "Yes, Will, I suppose I should try even harder to be nice to her."

Will grinned.

"But do me a favor—no more of that 'Lana Healey' stuff, okay?"

"Okay, Gregory."

LANA WAS WIPING TABLES, her mind rearranging the bits of property in question like a jigsaw puzzle that seemed to have no matching pieces, when the bell on the door rang. She'd grown accustomed to the bizarre jerk of her heart each time she looked up with the notion that Greg Healey would stride in bearing an olive branch.

But while the man who walked in was about the same age and pleasing to look at, he was no Greg Healey. His hair was auburn, his eyes bright blue, plus he was generous with his smile.

"I'm looking for Lana Martina."

She wiped her hands on a coffee-stained apron, and smiled in return. "You found her."

Another smile. "I'm Rich Enderling. I called about the ad for a roommate."

Lana brightened, and gestured for him to sit. She harbored hope that he would be the answer to one of her immediate problems, but she was wary. "Are you from around here?"

"No. I've been living in a small town in Mississippi for the past few years." His smile was sheepish. "I'm supposed to start a new job Monday, but the apartment I arranged for over the Internet is unlivable, so I'm driving around with a U-Haul and the *Attitude*'s want ads."

"What kind of job?" she asked warily. The last thing she needed was a live-in deadbeat.

"Product development with Phillips Foods. Are you familiar with the company?"

"Vaguely. My best friend's husband runs an advertising agency, and I think Phillips is one of his clients. They process honey or something?"

"Right."

"You don't look like a beekeeper."

He laughed. "I'm a food scientist, and Phillips is expanding into other product lines."

Lana perked up. "You cook?"

"Yes, some."

She bit back her excitement. This guy would be perfect...if he was of the requisite, um, *orientation*. Recalling Jack's comment about not inviting strange men back to her apartment until she knew what she was dealing with, she squinted, surveying Rich Enderling for...what? Color coordination? Good taste? The man looked great in chinos, T-shirt and a denim jacket. He smelled nice and...masculine. She sighed—if this man was gay, she couldn't tell. After all, she'd thought Greg Healey was gay, and look where *that* mistake had gotten her.

Leaning close, she lowered her voice conspiratorially. "Just one more thing before I show you the apartment."

Rich leaned forward, as well. "Yes?"

Lana grabbed him by the jacket collar and pulled his lips against hers for an experimental kiss. From her point of view, the kiss was pleasant—nice moisture, good firmness, with a full bouquet. But no zing, no electricity, no promise. Distantly she heard the bell on the door.

When Lana pulled back, Rich was wearing an amused smile. "I was under the impression you were looking for a *gay* roommate."

Satisfied, she grinned. "Don't move. I'll be right back." She stood and turned a bright smile in the direction of her customer, but faltered when she met Greg Healey's smirking gaze.

10

WHEN GREG WALKED into the coffee shop, a strange gnaw-
ing attacked his stomach. It could have been hunger pains
triggered by the wonderful aromas inside the shop, but he
had a sneaking suspicion the sensation had something to
do with seeing Lana Martina engaged in a kiss with the
man seated at the table. A "boyfriend" probably, from her
ad. After all, Coffee Girl was nationwide.

"Hi, Greg," she said, offering him a sunny smile. "This is
a surprise."

Obviously. He steeled himself against her powerful al-
lure, but she was radiant in a violet-colored sweater that
complemented her eyes. She didn't appear to be armed—
the guy at the table must be a better kisser.

Unreasonable anger sparked in him. "I was on my way
in to the office," he said in his boardroom voice, "and
thought I'd see if we could set up a time to meet."

"You're working on a Saturday?"

He wasn't in the mood for conversation—not with her
boyfriend watching from five feet away. Besides, he had to
bite his tongue to keep from telling her that her filibuster of
the rezoning proposal meant extra work for him. "Yes, I'm
working today. How about lunch?"

She looked regretful. "Lunch is one of my busiest times.
How about dinner, instead?"

"Dinner?" He tried to mask his surprise—and the unexpected flutter of pleasure.

"Oh, you probably already have plans."

"No," he said quickly, then recovered. "I mean, I'd like to get the ball rolling as soon as possible."

"Super—"

Her smile made his heart jump.

"Give me a minute to make sure someone can cover for me this evening."

Greg watched her disappear into the back room, hips swaying. Lust clutched his stomach—the woman had a fabulous rear view. When he made himself look away, the Kissing Man at the table gave him a knowing smile. Warmth crept up his neck. He acknowledged the man with a curt nod, then busied himself studying the large room.

The tables were surprisingly crowded. A funky, upbeat station played over the speakers on the drooping stage at the far end of the room. Students lounged on couches and in overstuffed chairs, pretending to study for upcoming final exams. They looked so young and carefree, he experienced a pang of envy. His own college years seemed like a lifetime ago, and not nearly so happy-go-lucky. In hindsight, his father's pressure to perform had chafed him like a saddle—

"Good news," Lana said behind him.

He dragged his mind back to the present.

"I can get away around eight for a couple of hours."

"Great," he said, almost smiling before he realized what he was doing. "How about Brady's?"

"I'll meet you there."

"I'll pick you up."

"No," she said sweetly. "I'll meet you there. Can I offer you a cappuccino—on the house?"

"I'll...I'll take a raincheck," he said, mesmerized by her eyes. "And I'll let you get back to—" he gestured toward Kissing Man "—work."

"Okay. Later," she said with a little wave.

Her smile stayed with him until he drove right past the parking garage for his office building. Since he'd already missed his turn, he somehow found his way down to the courthouse. The place would be relatively quiet on a Saturday.

He entered the echoing halls of the building, staring at the pictures of great judges who'd come before, dredging up memories of his collegiate aspirations. When the rumble of raised voices reached him, he followed the noise down a corridor where a trial was taking place. With his heart pounding in anticipation, Greg slipped inside the half-empty courtroom and took a seat on the back bench. Quickly he was transported from the world of contracts and hours-long conference calls into the cogs of the legal machine he had revered for as long as he could remember.

When the judge's gavel came down to adjourn court, Greg realized with a start that the entire afternoon had slipped away. The To Do list in his office seemed even more unappealing than it had this morning. With regret, he left the courtroom, but was infused with a powerful energy he hadn't experienced in ages. What a curious turn his life had taken in the past few days—Will's unexpected quest for a girlfriend, the prospect of financial freedom, and Lana Martina's peculiar intersection with both issues.

Somehow over the next few weeks he would win her over to his side. Perhaps he could appeal to the woman's sense of community obligation, or maybe…Greg pursed his mouth as Will's words over breakfast came back to him. *Be nice to her.* Maybe he could win her over the old-fashioned way. He puffed out his cheeks in a noisy exhale. And that meant he had to be charming. Damn.

Regardless, the sooner the rezoning proposal passed, the

sooner contracts with developers would be signed, and the closer he would be to spending his days in the courtroom.

When a brother's security and a person's own lifelong dreams were at stake, a man had to do what a man had to do.

"YOU'VE GOT YOURSELF a deal," Rich Enderling said.

Lana accepted his hand in a friendly shake and squealed. "You can't imagine how happy I am that this worked out."

Her new roommate gave her a teasing grin. "Isn't going from kissing to a handshake considered a step backward?"

A blush warmed her cheeks. "Sorry about that. I had to make sure that—well, you know."

"That I'm gay?"

She nodded.

"Hey, I was fine with the kiss, but I got the feeling that the guy in the coffee shop wasn't."

She frowned. "What guy?"

"Dark hair, Brooks Brothers clothes."

"Greg Healey?"

He smiled. "I didn't catch his name, and when I saw he only had eyes for you, I didn't bother."

Lana held up her hands. "Hold on. Greg Healey is the man trying to shut down my coffee shop by rezoning the property. The only thing he has eyes for is my unemployment."

He shrugged. "I guess I was wrong. I thought I saw some sort of history between you two. Listen, I need to take care of some things before I start unloading my stuff."

She was still pondering his observation. "Um, sure."

"Great. See you," he said on the way out the door.

Lana sighed in relief. At least one of her problems seemed resolved. Of course, there was that little matter left of saving her business.

FROM HIS SEAT AT A TABLE inside the bar at Brady's, Greg glanced out the window for the fiftieth time to catch sight of Lana Martina coming down the sidewalk. His finger tapped against his glass. The unplanned sojourn into the courtroom today had fueled his fever to practice law, and this rezoning project was his escape hatch from a lifetime of obligation. He did sympathize with the business owners who leased the property he owned, but this was, after all, the United States of America, where the person who owned the land was typically given a voice on what to do with it. He simply needed to neutralize—

He blinked as a red scooter zipped by, the helmeted driver wearing a telltale black-and-white spotted coat. Lana Martina pulled up to valet parking, put down the kickstand, hopped off, then removed her helmet. She said something to the suited valet before bounding toward the entrance. Greg shook his head in wonder, as the man climbed on gingerly and drove the cycle away.

She created a bit of a scene, walking into the upscale restaurant wearing that ridiculous coat, carrying a blue helmet and fluffing her pale hair. Desire, thick and heavy, pooled in his stomach.

"Hi," she said breathlessly. "Sorry I'm late."

With some effort, he dragged his tongue from the roof of his mouth. "Nothing serious, I hope."

"No, just a minor glitch at the shop."

Her cheeks glowed, her eyes shone—and his body reacted accordingly. Greg jerked his thumb toward the window. "Don't tell me that souped-up bicycle is your primary mode of transportation."

"It's a moped," she corrected him. "And if more people drove mopeds instead of gas-guzzling luxury cars, the city wouldn't have to worry about high auto emissions."

One corner of his mouth lifted. "Touché." He stared at

her, desire still throbbing inside him and wondered what about this woman spurred him to unusual behavior, then decided he didn't want to delve too deeply. "Our table is ready." Following her to the hostess station, Greg silently repeated his goal: to secure her cooperation.

"Check your coat?" he asked, then helped her out of the dalmatian look-alike garment.

"I'm afraid I'm underdressed," she said, looking around at the elegantly clad patrons. She smoothed a hand down the sleeve of the pink ruffled poet's blouse with a neckline so plunging that it stole the moisture from his mouth.

"You look great," he managed to say. Surely she was wearing a bra. With much effort, he tore his gaze from her cleavage. The rest of her slender body was clad in black jeans with embroidery running down one leg. Jingle-bell earrings with tiny green ribbons swung from her delicate earlobes. Her hair was arranged in that messy style that women were paying a lot of money for these days, although he suspected that Lana Martina might have been the person who started the look because it seemed so...*right* on her.

The sleek hostess apparently disagreed, based on the dubious glance she bestowed on Lana when Lana wasn't looking. At the woman's snub, protective feelings bloomed in his chest, much like when Will was slighted by others. Greg stepped closer to Lana, and his hand involuntarily snaked to her back. She stiffened, but he simply pressed her forward, the warm skin between her shoulder blades burning through the thin layer of fabric into his palm.

Greg summoned strength. The woman was playing dirty. She was definitely not wearing a bra.

11

HE MAINTAINED steady pressure against her back, while they threaded between round tables adorned with candles and flowers, and spaced for privacy. He liked touching her, but he suspected the feeling wasn't mutual.

"I knew this was a nice place," she said, as he pulled out her seat. "I just didn't realize *how* nice."

He acknowledged with a nod the white tablecloth, the fine crystal, the gleaming china. Orchestral holiday tunes floated around them. "Your first time here?"

She nodded, opening the menu. "This kind of place really isn't my bag. A little pricey for my budget."

"Dinner is my treat, of course," he said quickly.

"No, thank you. I'm not out of a job *yet*."

Greg frowned. "I'm not trying to put you out of a job."

She set aside her menu. "But that's exactly what will happen if the rezoning proposal passes as is. For me and a lot of other people."

He looked at her over the top of the wine list. "I was hoping we could have a nice meal before we got down to business."

She looked as if she were about to argue, then her expression changed. "You're right."

Her relenting smile coincided with the arrival of the waiter. "Something from the wine list, sir?"

"Split a bottle of pinot noir with me?" Greg asked her.

"Wine goes straight to my head," she said, then turned to the waiter. "Do you have cranberry juice?"

The man seemed surprised, then nodded.

Greg bit back a smile. "Then make that a carafe of pinot and a carafe of cranberry juice."

"Very good, sir. Would you like appetizers?"

Lana pressed her lips together, then shook her head.

Suspecting she was calculating the check in her head, Greg had the urge to order one of everything for her, but he swallowed words he knew she would resent and told the waiter he would pass, as well.

She sneaked a look at her watch, which had some kind of cartoon character on its face. "Would it be all right if we placed our entrée orders now?"

A tiny frown flitted across the waiter's face, but he acquiesced. Greg was vaguely disappointed that she was already anticipating the end of their date—er, meeting. Maybe she had something planned with the Kissing Man. She ordered pasta and roasted tomatoes; Greg opted for steak and asparagus.

"Are you a vegetarian?" he asked, when the waiter left.

"Reformed," she said.

"Meaning?"

"Meaning I don't eat red meat, but I don't like to wear plastic shoes, either."

He laughed in spite of himself. "And do you champion other causes?"

She gave him a self-deprecating smile. "Recycling, fuel conservation, water management, and a few others."

"Let me guess. You were in the Peace Corps?"

"No, as a matter of fact, I graduated from UK a few years behind you. Accounting and French."

Another surprise. "And how did accounting and French lead to owning a coffee shop?"

"I did my time at Ladd-Markham, then moved on to better things."

"Ladd-Markham?" He drew back. "Somehow I can't see you in a navy suit and starched white shirt."

"The seven longest years of my life. When the company offered severance packages a year ago, I jumped on it. Best Cuppa Joe had been a favorite hangout of mine since college, so when I found out it was for sale..." She shrugged. "It probably sounds crazy to you, leaving a high-powered corporate job to pursue something so esoteric."

A slow wonder crept over him, and his mouth went curiously dry. "You might be surprised."

Their drinks arrived, and Greg did the pouring honors while his head swam with new revelations. "A toast," he said, raising his glass. "To noble motivation."

He clinked his wineglass to her glass of cranberry juice.

Greg savored the dry wine on his tongue before swallowing. His senses seemed heightened, poised for stimulation. Lana unwittingly obliged with her intense eye contact.

"Speaking of motivation," she said, "what's yours regarding the rezoning project?"

Determined not to reveal how squarely she'd hit a nerve, he shrugged. "I want what's best for the city."

"And your bank account?" Her fingers slid up and down her glass in a caress.

"My *family's* bank account. And in this case, what's good for one is also good for the other. I'm running a business, the same as you."

"I wonder if it's the only thing we have in common," she said lightly.

Again their gazes connected, and the sight of her glowing in the candlelight stole the breath from Greg's lungs. The cranberry juice had stained her lips crimson. Her earrings tinkled when she moved. The memory of their kiss hit him again, and he was overwhelmed with the urge to touch her.

From inside his jacket pocket, his phone emitted a muted ring, breaking the moment. "Excuse me," he murmured, then withdrew the phone and glanced at the tiny display screen. "It's Will," he said. "Otherwise, I wouldn't bother."

"Would you like some privacy?"

He shook his head as he flipped open the mouthpiece. "Hey, buddy, what's up?"

"I'm sorry to bother you, Gregory. Are you busy?"

"As a matter of fact, I'm having a meeting with Ms. Martina."

"Really? I bet she looks pretty, doesn't she?"

He glanced across the table where Lana was buttering a roll. She discreetly licked the tip of her index finger, then blushed when she realized he'd caught her.

"Gregory, did you hear me?"

He cleared his throat. "Er, yes, Will. Yes, you're right. Did you need something?"

"Yvonne and I are decorating the Christmas tree, and I can't find the angel for the top. Do you know where it is?"

Greg smiled into the phone—Will and that angel. "When I was in the storage closet this summer, I believe it was on the top shelf, behind the ski equipment."

"Thanks, Gregory, I'll go look. But I'll wait until you get home before we put the angel on top."

"Sure, pal."

"Tell Lana hello for me. And don't forget—you're supposed to be nice to her."

"I will be. Goodbye."

"Goodbye, Gregory."

He hung up the phone, and accepted the bread basket Lana handed him.

"And how is Will?" she asked.

Her sincerity loosened his tongue. "He has a crush on you."

She grinned. "Ah, that's why he asked me the other evening if I had a boyfriend. He's a real gem."

"Yes," he said carefully. "I'd hate for him to be hurt by...anyone."

She tilted her head. "I could never hurt Will."

He could lose himself in her eyes. Did she realize the power she wielded with a flutter of those sooty lashes? "Maybe not intentionally, but he's more sensitive than most people."

"I could see that," she murmured. "There's quite an age difference between you, isn't there?"

"Ten years."

She smiled. "I suppose you've always looked out for him."

Sediment swirled in the bottom of his wineglass. "Except for the time he followed me up a tree and fell twenty feet to the ground—" As soon as the words were out of his mouth, he wanted them back. He never talked about the accident. When he lifted his gaze to see the sympathy in her eyes, he considered leaving.

"When was that?" she asked softly.

In for a penny, in for a pound. "I was fourteen, he was four." In the silence that followed, he drained his glass and refilled it.

"It wasn't your fault, Greg."

He manufactured a dry smile. "Will has said that a thousand times."

She smiled so deeply, that elusive dimple emerged. "He knows when you're hurting. You're very lucky to have Will for a brother."

Funny, but everyone had always said that Will was lucky to have *him*. Lana's words resounded in his heart. "Yes, I am." He squared his shoulders, grateful for the graceful exit she'd given him. "Do you have brothers and sisters?"

"No."

The one word reverberated with a sadness that surprised him. "Are your parents living?"

She nodded. "But they're divorced. My father moves around a lot, and Janet lives in Florida."

"Janet?"

Her laugh was self-conscious. "My mother looks young for her age, so she doesn't like to be called 'Mom.'"

So she had one of *those* mothers. Maybe that explained why Lana was so...complicated.

"But she's coming to spend an old-fashioned Christmas Eve with me." Her voice was childlike in her mother's defense. "How will you spend Christmas?"

He shrugged. "At home with Will and Yvonne." It was a quiet ritual he took for granted. If Will found a woman, all their routines would change—holidays, vacations, perhaps even living arrangements.

"Yvonne?" She seemed intent on removing a spot from the side of her glass.

"Our housekeeper. She was also a friend of my mother's."

"Oh. Your mother is deceased, too?"

He nodded.

"I'm so sorry," she murmured, her voice catching in such a way that he wished they hadn't ventured into personal territory. "You're very young to be alone."

"Well...I'm not alone," he said, flustered. "I mean, like you said, I have Will."

"And he has you."

"Yes."

"That's nice," she said, nodding. "Brothers should stick together. Have either of you ever been married?"

"No." He hadn't meant to sound so vehement. "You?"

A small smile lifted the corners of her mouth. "No. The single life suits me. I love my business, and I spend most of my free time on causes I believe in. I don't see marriage in my future."

One of those bald-faced lies that women told, he noted sardonically. Designed to trick a man into thinking he wasn't being silently measured for a tux. He decided to call her bluff. "If that's the case, then why would an attractive, successful woman like you place a singles ad?"

She stared at him for the longest time, her mouth pursing and unpursing, then she leaned her elbows on the table. "And why, Mr. Seriously Confirmed Bachelor, would an attractive, successful man like you answer one?"

Now he'd painted himself into a corner. Once again he considered telling her the truth—that he'd been checking her out for Will. Now that she'd met Will, surely she would understand his motives. But if he admitted he'd gone on Will's behalf, wouldn't he also have to admit that he'd chucked his brotherly concern in the face of his raging libido? Debating the lesser of two evils, Greg chose silence.

And by some miracle, their food arrived to relieve the awkward lapse.

She was either just as hungry as he, or just as reluctant to revisit the subject of their first meeting, because she ate in relative silence, dividing the black olives from her pasta into a forlorn little pile on the side of her plate.

"I take it you don't like olives?"

She blushed like a schoolgirl. "Well, I don't lie awake thinking about them, no."

He leaned one elbow on the table. "What *do* you lie awake thinking about?"

She played with the stem of her glass. "Oh, the usual— world peace and clean air."

"Seriously?"

She nodded. "Sometimes." She smiled into her drink. "And sometimes I lie awake thinking about people I care about, wondering what they're doing."

He held his breath, wondering who belonged in that privileged circle.

She turned a pointed look in his direction. "And sometimes I lie awake thinking about meeting my business loan payments."

Greg lifted his glass. "Then it's safe to say we lie awake thinking about the same things. Sometimes." Of course, for the past couple of nights he'd lain awake thinking about her.

Lana pushed aside her half-empty plate and withdrew a notepad from her purse, the pages crammed with handwriting. "I have to relieve an employee in an hour, so if you don't mind..." She leaned forward, inadvertently giving him a gut-clutching glimpse inside her pink blouse.

He dropped his napkin in his plate. "I'm looking—er, listening."

Her smile was conciliatory. "First of all, I don't deny that I'm trying to save my business," she said. "But I also don't want to see the character of the downtown area sacrificed for cookie-cutter condos and town homes."

He refilled both of their glasses. "The residential area doesn't have to be cookie-cutter. And I don't think you're looking at the proposal objectively."

"Well, if that isn't the pot calling the kettle black."

He attributed her seductive laugh to the fact that he'd drunk too much wine. Greg's frustration climbed, partly because they were getting nowhere, and partly because it was the first time in months he'd had dinner with a beautiful woman, and they were talking business. "You'd prefer that I let my investment decay?"

"Of course not. The timing is lousy, but I'm glad the subject has been raised. You see, *I* live in the city, so I have a vested interest in what happens to it."

"Yes, but *I* own property in the city, so I have more of a vested interest."

She cocked her head at him. "Is that so? Do you shop in Hyde Parkland?"

He shifted in his seat. "Occasionally."

Her laugh was dubious. "The day we met was the first time you'd even been inside my shop, wasn't it."

"Yes."

"And can you tell me what is on either side of my shop?"

He squinted, trying to remember, but it was so hard to concentrate when she was looking at him like that, her eyes on fire, her color heightened. And that blouse—good grief, he was only human. "I don't remember."

She leaned back in her chair, shaking her head. "I don't believe this. You're not even familiar with your own property?"

"The company owns dozens of parcels of property. I can't be expected to know about each one in detail."

"Oh, really?" Wearing a conspiratorial smile, Lana waved her hand and called, "Waiter, our checks, please."

"But we're not finished," Greg said, gesturing to his wineglass. In truth, he wasn't ready for the evening to end. Not even close.

"We're finished here," she assured him. "Drink up. I'm taking you on a little tour."

12

"I DON'T BELIEVE I'm doing this," Greg said near her ear.

Lana laughed at his self-consciousness. "Just try to blend. If the police see that you're not wearing a helmet, you'll get a ticket."

"Oh, great. Why can't we just go in my car?"

"The gas-guzzler?"

"Dad left the Mercedes to Will. I drive a..."

"A what?"

"A Porsche," he muttered. "But it gets decent gas mileage," he added, as if the car's fuel economy made up for its obscene price tag.

Lana threw a smirk over her shoulder. "Slumming will be good for you."

"I feel ridiculous."

"Relax," she said. "You *look* ridiculous, too. Hang on."

Not that the moped had an engine that would tear a person's head off, but balancing could be a bit tricky riding double. She goosed the gas, and after an initial protest at the unaccustomed load, the cycle chugged forward. Carefully, she pulled from the parking lot onto the quiet, dark side street, and soon they were humming along at top speed—around thirty miles an hour—with a nippy wind blowing over them. Her cheeks stung and her eyes watered, but the night riding exhilarated her. At least she *thought* it was the night riding that had her blood pumping so efficiently.

"This is as fast as the thing goes?"

"What do you expect?"

"Somebody could practically run up beside you and have a conversation."

"Another plus," she agreed.

He was hanging on to the bar behind the seat, but his body was tucked up close around hers, emanating warmth she consciously had to avoid sinking back into. At the first light she stopped for, he put his feet down to help her steady the bike. But when the light turned, their push-off was so uncoordinated, Greg lost a shoe. Turning the moped around was difficult because her arms were weak from laughing. He, on the other hand, had an expression that would have rivaled the Grinch's.

"Careful, your face will get stuck that way," she chided, as he leaned over to scoop up his shoe.

If possible, his scowl deepened.

"Of course, in your case," she continued dryly, "it might save you time in future." She zoomed off the minute he slid the shoe onto his foot, gratified at the yelp he gave before he got a handhold.

Laughter bubbled in her stomach. The dour man was so easy to provoke, and doing so gave her the most wicked sense of delight. But even as she smiled to herself, mixed feelings coursed through her—a faint pang of disappointment that this man seemed too stiff and unwieldy to enjoy simple pleasures, and relief that if not for The Best Cuppa Joe, she might still be rooted in a job she hated, with the same narrow view of the world: cynical and clinical. Holy high heels.

But even though she carried a reluctant passenger tonight, the streets were beautiful, awash with twinkling lights and strung with banners heralding the holiday season. The air was as cool as peppermint in her throat and lungs. People moved along the sidewalks in clusters, leaving restaurants and visiting shops that had extended their hours for Christmas. On impulse, she detoured a few blocks to buzz by Tremont's department store and take in the lit window displays—looping trains and animated dolls and spinning tricycles. Pure magic.

"My father brought me here every year to look in the windows when I was little," Lana said, slowing at the corner to relive the memories.

"Mine, too," he said, his voice thick.

Surprised at his admission, she tried to imagine Greg as a child. Solemn, brooding, temperamental. "And afterward, we'd have hot cider from a street cart," she added.

"With cinnamon sticks to stir."

His words triggered a smile. "Yes!" How extraordinary that they shared a memory. But when she turned her head to say so, his face was closer than she'd expected. The wind had whipped his dark hair over his forehead, concealing the furrows there. Her pulse picked up at the glimpse of a more carefree Greg Healey. A faint smile licked at the corners of his strong mouth. Then his eyes went wide.

"*Watch out!*"

She jerked her attention back to the road and swerved to avoid a metal trash can that had rolled into the street. They nearly wiped out, but Greg saved the day by assuming their weight, first on one foot then the other, as she fought for control. Finally Lana yanked the cycle toward the curb and braked to a stop. They promptly fell over, bike and all, spilling onto the sidewalk, a knot of arms and legs and handlebars. She lay still for a few seconds, taking stock of her limbs and joints. Actually, the impact hadn't been that bad.

A grunt sounded beneath her, explaining *why* the impact hadn't been that bad. "Are you all right?" she asked.

"I will be when you get off me," he muttered, his voice menacingly calm.

She was suddenly very aware of his big, firm body beneath hers, warm and accommodating. The sensation wasn't wholly unpleasant, but she couldn't very well lie there enjoying it when the man obviously didn't share her opinion. She flailed her arms, but her efforts were futile in the bulky coat. Beneath her, his body jerked, and she realized she heard laughter. The shocking sound started her laughing, too, and their voices blended in the clear air.

"You folks need a hand?"

She sobered and looked up into the face of a middle-aged stranger. "Uh, no. No, thank you."

The man shook his head and moved on.

She burst into giggles and tried again to get up, but succeeded only in grinding her body against his—to noticeable effect. Finally, Greg grabbed her arms and rolled her off his body.

She stopped laughing when she realized he was practically on top of her now. His head was bent close, and his torso covered hers. His labored breath puffed out in little white clouds. Hers might have, if it hadn't been trapped in her chest. Lust stabbed her low and hard. Shadows swathed his face, but his eyes glinted with...desire? Her lips parted, and she realized that she wanted him to kiss her again. He swallowed audibly. The absurdity of the situation was overridden by the unmistakable chemistry that resonated between them, even when heavily clothed, helmeted and lying on freezing pavement.

"Are you okay?" he finally asked, his voice a bit unsteady.

"I think so." If she could think. "You?"

"I think so." He pushed himself up, rubbed his shoulder, then extended his hand to help her. His fingers were long and strong and warm, even through her thin driving gloves. The passionate moment lingered between them. Confusion clogged her mind because she couldn't reconcile her dislike of the person with her attraction to the man.

"I—I'm sorry about, um, crashing." She thought it wise not to mention the source of her distraction. "I'm not used to having another person along."

But if possible, his eyes grew even more serious. "That makes two of us."

She realized with a start that His Uptightness was being philosophical on a cold night standing in the middle of a sidewalk. She didn't like this side of him because it... messed up her plans.

Averting her gaze, Lana noticed a tear in the sleeve of his suit jacket. "Oh, no, your jacket is ripped." She fingered the expensive fabric, seized by a curiously domestic urge to fix it.

He glanced down and brushed his hand over the tear, then grinned. "Do you realize that I've walked away from every encounter with you bearing a battle wound? I can't decide if you're bad luck or if you're trying to get rid of the competition."

She managed a grin as she tightened the strap on her helmet. "I think I'll keep you guessing. I am sorry about the jacket, though. I'll have it repaired."

"That's not necessary," he said, righting her moped with one hand.

"No, really," she said as she straddled the bike. "I have this employee who's a whiz with a needle and thread." It was Annette's fault that she and Greg had gotten off to such a rotten start in the first place. "Believe me, she owes me one."

He was standing with his arms crossed.

"Aren't you going to get on?"

"I don't think so."

"Oh, come on, I'll be extra careful."

He shook his head. "Not unless I can drive."

"What? No way."

"Yes way. I'm driving, or I take a taxi back to the restaurant."

Lana frowned and looked around. They were only about four blocks away from her shop. "Okay," she said, climbing off to give him access to the handlebars. "But if you demolish my bike, you have to provide me with another mode of transportation."

"I'm sure Will would loan you his horse," he said, his voice almost teasing, except the man didn't tease. He threw one long leg over the moped, turned the key and wrapped his big hands around the grips.

"I'm afraid of horses," she said with a little laugh. He looked preposterous, twice as big as the bike, dressed in suit and tie, his legs winged out to the sides. She climbed on behind him, her mood lighter than in recent memory. "But I might take that little Porsche until my bike got out of the shop."

"Hypocrite," he said over his shoulder.

"Bully."

"Hang on."

He accelerated so quickly, she grabbed his waist, and when he didn't resist, she leaned into his warmth to give him directions. "Turn here. Okay, go straight." He had a few problems changing gears, and he was heavy on the brakes, but they moved along at a fairly consistent pace and finally reached the Hyde Parkland section.

"Slow down," she urged, and he slowed until the bike was barely moving. "There's Marshall Ballou's place. He was at the council meeting. Marsh has built quite a following."

"Used clothing?" he asked, his voice dubious.

"Vintage clothing," she corrected. "Just another way to recycle. Over there is Vic's Barber Shop. He's been in that location for longer than you and I have been alive."

He grunted acknowledgment. They wound around a couple more streets, dodging cars illegally parked.

"And over there is Paige Hollander's gift shop—she has a herb garden in the back where she serves sandwiches and tea. And two doors up is Maxie Dodd's bakery—she makes the best sourdough in town. I'll bet the restaurant where we ate tonight buys their dinner rolls from Maxie."

She pointed out another half-dozen mom-and-pop shops before they turned onto Hunt Street and headed toward her own business. "There's a rare-books store on one side of my shop, and a T-shirt business on the other side. Do you mind if I stop by my shop to check on things before taking you back to your car? It'll give us a chance to talk, too."

"Fine with me. I could use a hot cup of coffee."

Too late, she realized she'd have to let Annette in on her plan to butter up Greg Healey. Otherwise, the woman might take one look at him and decide that he wasn't a loser, after all, then spill the beans that *she* was Coffee Girl and *they* were destined to be together.

He wheeled into a tight spot and came to a too-abrupt stop, jamming her up against his shoulder blades. "Sorry," she murmured, tingling with awareness.

He turned his head. "I'm not."

They were still for an agonizing few seconds. To her dismay, she didn't want to let go, didn't want their intimate ride to end. In that split second, she wished she and Greg weren't embroiled in a sticky business fray—but things were what they were. Besides, the complications forced her to maintain a respectable distance from a man who was completely wrong for her. He'd seemed duly unimpressed with the causes she thought were important.

Lana eased back and dismounted, then quickly secured the cycle, her heart still pounding over his provocative statement. *I'm not.* Hadn't Alex warned her about letting her lust lead her astray?

While walking inside, she chided herself—she couldn't afford to become emotionally involved; she just needed him to ease up on the rezoning issue. Just a little flirting. *Maybe* a kiss or two.

He held open the door the way her father used to—so she'd have to pass under his arm. The gesture made her feel strangely protected, but she didn't have long to savor it. Her jaw dropped to see her friend Alex working behind the counter, her mussed hair and flushed face indicative of her frazzled state. "Alex, what are you doing here?"

Alex put a hand to her chest. "Thank goodness, you're back."

"Where's Annette?" Lana asked as she automatically grabbed an apron and slid behind the counter.

"Her ankle swelled up like a balloon. She called me, thinking I might know where you'd gone, and I told her I'd fill in." She blew her bangs straight up. "I hope I didn't scare away any customers."

"Don't be silly. Thanks, Alex. I should've told Annette where I'd be."

"And where were you?" her friend asked, her voice low and laced with innuendo as she glanced toward Greg, then back. "Working the man into a lather?"

"Shh. Here he comes." She smiled at him, struck anew by his dark good looks. "Greg Healey, meet my best friend, Alex Stillman."

"Nice to meet you," he said smoothly. "Weren't you at the council meeting last night?"

"Yes," Alex said, then smacked Lana on the back. "Wasn't Lana great? She's very smart, you know. She's a member of Mensa—*ow!*"

Lana patted the skin where she'd just inflicted a pinch on her friend's arm. "Thanks, Alex. I'm sure Jack is wondering where you are."

The corners of Greg's mouth twitched. "You're the one who married Jack the Attack Stillman. I remember him from UK."

"He remembers you, too," Alex said in a saccharine-sweet tone. "Except he used other letters when he talked about you—*ow!*"

Lana pasted on a smile and jerked her head toward the door. "Say *good-night*, Alex."

Her friend smirked and removed her apron. "Good night. Call me when you get a chance?" Alex's voice was high and unnatural.

She shot her an exasperated look. "Yes. Don't worry about me."

"Oh, I won't," Alex said loudly as she walked from behind the counter. "Because I know you have a black belt and you can take care of yourself."

Lana could only stare at her lying friend until Alex had walked out the door.

Greg walked to the counter and lifted an eyebrow. "Mensa?"

"Don't listen to her," she said with a laugh. "Alex must have drunk too much caffeine while she was here."

One corner of his mouth went back, and he jerked his thumb toward the door. "Listen, you're busy. I'll just take a taxi back to my car."

Her heart quickened as Greg took a tentative step backward. She realized with awful clarity that she didn't want him to leave, and that while saving her business should have been uppermost in her mind, it wasn't. "Wait!"

He stopped.

She conjured up a shaky smile. "I close in less than an hour, if you want to stick around. Maybe we'll get a quiet moment to...talk."

He looked back at the door, hesitating. Lana's heart thumped in her chest. Maybe he didn't feel the same push-pull sensation when their bodies came within ten feet of each other. Maybe he thought she was a kook, and wanted to return to his own kind. Heck, maybe she *was* a kook.

"Okay," he said with a shrug. "I'll stay."

Her friend Alex probably would have declared the little jolt of happiness Lana experienced at his response, which was casual at best, a sign of desperate loneliness. Thank goodness, Alex wasn't around.

13

GREG TOOK IN THE BUSTLING SHOP—customers sitting and standing, laughing and talking over the music of two acoustic guitarists flanked by no fewer than four Christmas trees on the cramped little stage. Miles of lights twinkled from the rafters. Aromas of coffee and chocolate and sugar filled his lungs. The place had charm, all right. Then he looked back to Lana Martina, tousled and red-cheeked and electric.

She was the charm. People gravitated toward her. *He* gravitated toward her. The realization hit him hard, and he tried to rationalize his irrational feelings. He wasn't completely immune to the sappiness of the holidays. And her wild sense of adventure was simply a passing intrigue. Still, this...*attraction* would make his task of winning her over to his side a bit easier, and much more pleasurable.

So why did he have the feeling that when he'd said "I'll stay," he was committing to something much larger?

Her smile erased his concern. "Good. What can I get you to drink?"

"Decaf, black."

"What kind?"

"What kind what?"

"What kind of decaf?" She pointed to the menu behind her that listed as least thirty different types of bean blends, several of them decaf.

He shrugged. "Pick one."

She plunked a fuzzy Santa hat on her head, the same one she'd been wearing when he first met her. "How about our special holiday blend?"

"As long as it's hot."

The drink appeared in front of him within thirty seconds, then she returned to her customers. He sipped his coffee, which was surprisingly good, and took advantage of the time to study her. She moved efficiently behind the bar, taking orders and dispensing beverages while bantering with patrons. Her profile was exquisite, both above and below the neck. She was finely boned, richly curved and eminently appealing. Gripped by a strong urge to have her, he was reminded that the woman already had a man in her life. There was The Kissing Man, and possibly others. He didn't relish being one in a long line of her classified-ad lovers.

Yet he knew if the opportunity presented itself, he'd dive headfirst into her bed.

In an attempt to distract himself from his unexplainable fixation with the woman, he left the bar to read the items posted on the enormous bulletin board along the wall leading to the rest rooms. Flyers were posted for typing services, cars for sale, and dog-sitting. Plus a half-dozen petitions were posted for saving the rain forest, preventing animal abuse and other causes.

Greg shook his head because the people who had signed the petitions were fooling themselves if they thought a mere signature would change the shape of things. If they really wanted to make a difference, they'd do something concrete. In his experience, only money—the incentive to make it, or not to lose it—had the power to influence change. Couldn't Lana see that the best chance for solving the world's problems lay in commerce, not in caring?

No, which demonstrated how fundamentally oppositely he and she were wired.

"Lana!"

At the sound of her name over the microphone, Greg turned to see the two young male singers beckoning her toward the stage.

"Come and lead us in a song."

Despite the chorus of encouragement, she shook her head and held up her hands to decline. "I can't sing!"

But the cheers grew louder, and Greg joined in. She glanced at him, her cheeks bright red, and he realized with a start that she cared what he thought. He jerked his head toward the stage and mouthed, *Chicken*.

The correct word choice, judging by the sudden lift of her chin. She marched up to the stage, conferred with the musicians, then led the room in a rousing rendition of "I Wanna Hippopotamus for Christmas." Her voice was horrifically off-key, but loud and enthusiastic as she conducted a crowd that was on a cumulative caffeine buzz. Greg found himself smiling into his hand. Despite his dare, he marveled at her nerve. No amount of money, much less plain goading, would have gotten him on that stage. But she was a sport, bouncing around like a child, acting out the song like a vaudeville entertainer.

The applause was thunderous, and he joined in goodnaturedly. She glanced his way and delivered a little salute, then reminded everyone that one of the trees on the stage was decorated with tags bearing the name of a needy boy or girl and his or her Christmas wish list. "Help make this year special for one child who might not otherwise have any gifts at all."

Greg drained his coffee cup. Good grief, she'd turned the place into her own little do-good center. Still, guilt stirred in his stomach at the sight of the tree she indicated, covered with name tags, each representing a child. Others must have felt the same guilt, because as she left the stage, the tree was surrounded by customers. The guitarists extended the spirited mood with more holiday songs.

And for a moment, Greg *almost* bought into the whole Christmas spirit thing. But a more sensible part of him stubbornly resisted. What good did it do to be kind to your fellow man a couple of weeks out of the year? To participate in hand-out programs that made the giver feel good, and the recipient feel pitied? Lana Martina was a comely ambassador, perky and persuasive. But one woman wouldn't change his entire mode of thinking. Even if she was compelling. And braless.

Still, he conceded a proprietary thrill when she left the stage and made her way toward him, as if they were together. The woman was certainly more interesting than most of the women he'd dated. But interesting translated to one thing: complicated.

"You're multitalented," he observed, when she stopped in front of him.

"If I didn't know better, I'd think that was a compliment."

He lifted his coffee cup. "But you know better."

"Yes, I do. Need a refill?"

"Sure." He followed her to the bar, confounded by his urge to be near her. She yanked on a red cord, which rang a bell he was sure could be heard all the way to Louisville.

"Last call!" she bellowed.

Greg blinked. Last call in a coffee shop?

One by one, the customers unfolded themselves from their comfortable seats, most of them sauntering to the counter for half-cup refills, although a few collected their coats from the long row of hooks along one wall. Those leaving called good-night to Lana, and she knew each person by name. A half hour later, the two musicians, who were the last to leave, waved and carried their acoustic guitars out the front door. Lana locked the door behind them, and pulled down the blinds. She flipped knobs on an old metal switch plate to extinguish the lights over the door and windows, then turned an ancient sign from *Come on in* to *Sorry, we're closed*. At long last, they were alone. His vital signs increased, and longing pooled in his belly.

She began to clear the tables. "This shouldn't take long, then we can talk."

Greg remained glued to the padded stool, turning to watch her as unobtrusively as possible. She bussed the tables with remarkable energy, humming as she dumped trash into a compartmentalized bin she wheeled around. The woman had a fabulous figure.

"Was the crowd typical for a Saturday night?" he asked. It was more difficult to ogle while talking.

"Most evenings are decent when classes are in session. Otherwise, night business is dead. I'd love to see something open downtown to draw people out of the suburbs after five o'clock."

"Like what?"

She stopped and shrugged. "Like a planetarium."

He pursed his mouth. "Not a bad idea."

"I have others."

Be nice to her. "So let's hear them."

She dragged a canvas bag from beneath the counter and extracted the notebook he recognized from the restaurant. "Okay, but first a question. Why not just zone some of the buildings in question commercial and some residential?"

A legitimate question—from a layperson. "Property values will be more stable if the areas are blocked off separately rather than intermixed. Who wants to live next to a bar, for instance?"

She sighed. "And who wants to operate a business where customers have to fight for parking spaces?"

"Exactly."

"But it's pretty common in downtown areas to see storefronts on the first floor of a building, and condos or apartments above." She pointed to her ceiling. "There's an enormous attic in this building large enough for two apartments."

He smiled patiently. "*After* retrofitted plumbing and wiring. And adding handicapped access. And don't forget about the parking problems around here. To support allday, permanent parking needed for employees and customers and residents, you're looking at a parking garage."

She smirked. "So why does the parking garage have to go *here*?"

"Because the architects and engineers said so." At her frustrated sigh, he plunged on. "Listen, Lana, contrary to popular belief, this rezoning plan is not some kind of whimsical conspiracy to evict the shop owners of Hyde Parkland. My company has been working on this project for months, even years on some aspects. This is a huge undertaking that will, whether you want to believe it or not, give a much-needed boost to the downtown economy." He splayed his hands and lowered his voice to reflect his sympathy. "Unfortunately, there are always casualties of progress."

She shook her head stubbornly. "But this business has been here for thirty years! Doesn't that count for something?"

He pressed his lips together, then chose his words carefully. "Yes. It means something to you and to your customers. But if you'll be honest with yourself, you'll realize this area needs a parking garage more than it needs a coffee shop."

She averted her eyes and bit into her lower lip. She didn't seem like the crying type, but a man never knew. He watched her nervously, poised to whip out a clean hanky if she erupted. She didn't. He realized as he had before that the only other person in the world who evoked these protective feelings in him was Will. Not a good realization, considering that protecting Lana Martina's interests ran counter to protecting his own interests. And Will's.

Still, he felt compelled to say something healing. "Um, about that planetarium—maybe I'll look for a suitable piece of land and try to interest a developer."

She lifted her gaze. Sure enough, her violet eyes were falsely bright. "A lot of good a planetarium will do me when my coffee shop is a parking garage."

"Why don't you simply move your shop?"

"There isn't a location in town that would bring me the same amount of traffic."

Had he imagined that her voice broke on the last word? "How about your friend Alex's property, beneath Tremont's department store?"

"It's not *Alex's* property, and I can't afford the space."

"Surely she has enough pull to cut you slack on the rent."

From the set of her mouth, he'd hit a nerve.

"Alex offered. But I have this little hang-up about doing things on my own."

They were nearly eye to eye, and he was mesmerized by her beauty—her flawless skin, her unusual eyes, her plump mouth. Her work perfume of coffee beans and sugar and cinnamon tickled his nose. The woman had spunk, and sex appeal in spades.

"Funny," he said, reaching out to clasp her wrist, "so do I." He tested her resistance, pulling gently. She blinked, then came into his arms.

"What about the other shop owners?" she asked quietly. "Can you help them?"

"For you," he murmured, "I will certainly try."

Greg drew her into the cradle between his knees for a slow, thorough kiss, while alarms sounded in his head. What had he promised? What was this woman doing to him? She seemed tentative at first, but he beckoned her tongue with his and drew her into his intensity. Overwhelmed with the urge to devour her, his sex hardened to the point of pleasure-pain. He pressed his legs together, capturing her, drawing her heat closer to his. He wrapped his arms around her narrow waist, splaying his hands across her back. A whisper of fabric lay between his fingers and her warm skin. Her unbound breasts bore into his chest, and he groaned against the tide of desire that flooded his limbs.

He wanted her. Badly.

14

LANA WAS GLAD for his strength—her own had vanished. She was emotionally wrung, and Greg's arms gave her a place to escape the pressures weighing on her head. Just one kiss, she promised herself. They were finally talking, and he seemed somewhat sympathetic to the shop owners. He would help them, he would help her.

But thoughts of rezoning plans and parking garages and loan payments dissolved as the kiss matured into uncontrollable desire. She matched his parlaying tongue, stroke for stroke. When he slipped his hands beneath her blouse and skimmed the indention of her spine, she shuddered and moaned into his mouth. His lips slid to her neck, licking and kissing her throat. She leaned her head back and drove her fingers into his dark hair. He slid his hands forward and thumbed the undersides of her breasts, sending moisture to the juncture of her thighs. She cried out, and the shock of hearing her own voice echo off the brick walls restored a small measure of sanity.

"Greg," she said, her voice thick.

He mumbled an incoherent response against her collarbone.

"Greg, someone might see us."

He lifted his head, but maintained his hold on her. "Then let's go somewhere. To your place."

She opened her mouth to say yes, then remembered that

Rich Enderling was still moving his things in and shook her head. "No. It's...complicated."

"Lana, I want you." And he upped the ante by brushing his thumbs over the stiff peaks of her breasts.

Her shoulders rolled involuntarily as pleasure coursed through her chest and arms. She was powerless to speak. In one movement, he lifted her and spun on the stool, setting her on the cool wooden bar. His eyes were level with her tingling breasts, his arms encircling her and his hands cupping her bottom as if he were afraid she would try to pull away.

She didn't. The blinds were pulled and the lights were low. Anyone nosy enough to peek inside deserved the eyeful they got. His eyes were glazed with passion—passion for her. The knowledge that she was able to move this staid man filled her with an incredible surge of feminine power. Was there anything more sexy than pure enthusiasm?

"I want you, too," she whispered, and pulled his face to her breasts. He nipped at the aching tips, suckling through the gauzy cloth, wetting the pink fabric. She strained into him, luxuriating in the feel of his warm tongue against her sensitive zones. Kneading his shoulders through his starched shirt, she hungered to feel his bare skin.

Lana tugged at his loosened tie, then rapidly undid as many buttons as she could reach. Springy black hair met her fingers above a white ribbed undershirt that clung to smooth chest muscles. She fumbled with the buttons on his cuffs and helped him shrug out of the shirt, while he feasted on her breasts. When his dress shirt, undershirt and tie hit the floor, he stood and lifted her blouse over her head.

Perched on the edge of the bar and bare to the waist, she allowed him to look at her, and she looked back, wetting her lips at the sight of superbly defined shoulders, biceps, pectorals. When she'd had her fill, she lifted her gaze to his hooded one, and trembled at the promise she saw there. Intensity. Endurance. Satisfaction.

"You are exquisite," he murmured, his eyes shining.

Lana wrapped her legs around his waist and looped her arms around his neck before lowering her mouth to his. Something pulled at the back of her mind, a vague uneasiness that she shouldn't be doing what she was doing—but at the moment she couldn't fathom why. His body had been speaking to hers all evening.

With a groan, he pulled her off the bar and carried her across the darkened room. Her Santa hat fell off somewhere along the way. She wasn't certain of his destination until his lips left hers and she felt velour upholstery at her back. She smiled up at him and sank into the soft worn cushions of one of the vintage couches, anticipating the weight of him, the breadth of him, the length of him. Everything was perfect at the moment. Tomorrow would take care of itself.

A loud chiming sounded, startling her because she had to pull herself so far out of her real-life fantasy to decipher its source.

Greg's brow lowered. "What is it?"

She sat up and crossed her arms over her breasts. "The bell on the back door. I'm supposed to meet someone." She suddenly remembered.

"They'll leave," Greg said, reaching for her.

"No. He'll come around the front and see my moped. And he's liable to call the police if I don't answer the door."

"He?" Greg asked, his voice suspicious. "A boyfriend?"

Shame enveloped her as she stared at him. *A* boyfriend, as in one of many? Is that what he thought of her—that she had many men? Lana stood and brushed by him to scoop up her blouse. And why wouldn't he think the worst?

Hadn't she allowed him to believe she'd placed that singles ad? Hadn't she planned to lead him on, to cajole him into seeing her side of the rezoning matter? Of course, she'd never meant for things to go so far. A kiss, maybe two...

Lana jerked the blouse over her head to the tune of more insistent chiming from the back door. "He's a friend," she said through clenched teeth. "An artist who comes by every week to pick up colored glass I save."

He scoffed. "You've got to be kidding."

At the condescending look on his face, she swallowed the lump of disappointment that formed in her throat. She bent to retrieve his clothes so he wouldn't notice that what had almost happened had almost meant something to her, or that his opinion of her mattered. "Get dressed," she said.

GREG PULLED HIS UNDERSHIRT over his head and watched her walk away, feeling more empty and powerless than in recent memory. The interruption had frustrated him beyond logic. And reminded him that Lana dated lots of men. Plus, the woman had so damn many projects. He dragged his hand down over his face and exhaled noisily. Cripes, the woman was so...complicated.

Muttering to himself, he yanked on his dress shirt, then hastily buttoned the front and rolled up the cuffs. He looked for his jacket, then remembered she'd absconded with it to have it repaired, and sighed noisily. He hadn't planned for things to go so far, but he'd given in to the incredible attraction to her that ratcheted higher every time they were together. Now he was in worse shape than before. Greg unzipped his pants, adjusted his still rigid erection and tucked in his shirt. God, he'd never wanted a woman so much. The image of her sitting on the counter, bare-breasted, would forever be burned in his brain. They were both grown, consenting adults—what was the harm?

He sighed, massaging his neck. The rezoning plan was the harm. The rezoning plan that was supposed to breeze through the council and save downtown Lexington and set him free, all in one fell swoop. And now one little woman stood in his way. Lana Martina tripped his conscience not because she was right, but because she *thought* she was right. God save him from a hot-blooded do-gooder.

The murmur of voices floated to him from the back; then he heard a terrific clattering of glass as several boxes must have changed hands. He shook his head, then his gaze drifted to the Christmas tree with tags bearing the names of the children Lana had talked about earlier. Idly, he turned over one of the tags.

Joey, age 5, would like tennis shoes, size eleven.

Greg frowned. Shoes? Kids were supposed to get trucks and dolls and bikes for Christmas, not shoes. He turned over another tag. *Warm coat.* And another. *Books.*

He swore softly under his breath, stole a glance toward the back door, then yanked off the remaining tags and stuffed them into his pants pockets. Straightening self-consciously, he strode to the phone to call a taxi—a return trip on the moped would probably be somewhat less enjoyable than the one here. Besides, he didn't want Lana to ride back from the restaurant alone since it was getting late. He was just returning the receiver when he heard her call goodbye and the back door close.

She barely glanced at him when she returned, walking straight to a pan of dirty ceramic mugs sitting on one of the tables. "Give me a couple of minutes to clean up, then I'll take you back to your car."

"I called a taxi."

"Suit yourself." Her movements were rapid and jerky. "Tomorrow I'll call Ms. Wheeler and let her know that you and I can't work together on this plan, after all. Didn't you say you had a manager who would be more—"

"Lana." He walked up behind her, catching a whiff of her womanly scent, itching to touch her again. He knew instantly that despite the danger of becoming involved with her, he didn't want to turn the project over to someone else. "What just happened...it won't happen again."

She stopped working, but she didn't turn around. "Greg, 'what just happened' aside, you don't really care about me or any of the other business owners down here. You've lost touch with the community you're supposed to be helping. This situation is going nowhere."

He hated the droop of her shoulders, and the muted tone of her voice. He longed for the good-natured banter they'd shared earlier in the evening. "What would it take to convince you that I do care about...the business owners?"

Lana turned to face him and crossed her arms. "I don't know. Spend some time with them, talk to them. Maybe you'll come to realize how important they are to the downtown economy." Then she dismissed him with a wave of her hand. "Forget it, you won't get that close to real people."

"*Real* people? What's that supposed to mean?"

Her laugh mocked him. "You figure it out."

Greg straightened, irritated by her words. "I'm not afraid of getting close to...any kind of people."

She bent down to scoop up the Santa hat that had fallen off when he carried her to the couch, then she tossed it into the pan of dirty dishes. "Prove it."

He stared at the hat. Had she so casually dismissed what had almost happened? "How?"

"Tomorrow afternoon. Come down, tie on an apron, and walk a day in my shoes. Then we'll go around and meet the other shop owners."

An emphatic "no" hovered in the back of his throat, but he swallowed it when he looked into her violet eyes. After all, subsequent to that embarrassing display of physical weakness, he needed to initiate damage control. He still needed to win her over—if she told councilwoman Wheeler *why* they couldn't work together, who knew what kind of obstacles Wheeler could put in his way?

"I'll be here," he said.

15

"DID YOU SLEEP WELL?" Lana asked Rich, when he emerged from his bedroom looking scrubbed and spiffy in slacks and a turtleneck. She lay on her back beneath the Christmas tree, adjusting the tree stand to compensate for the substantial lean that had developed overnight. She knew exactly how the tree felt. Her world had certainly been knocked off-kilter these past few days.

"As a matter of fact, I did sleep well," her new roommate said, crouching near her. "Need some help?"

"Nope. I've got it." She gave the pliers one last turn, then wriggled out. "There."

Rich appraised the tree by tilting his head. "Is it supposed to be straight?"

"You mean it isn't?"

"My mistake—the tree's perfect." He stood. "And huge."

She smiled from her sitting position on the floor, gesturing to the mound of packages. "My mom is coming up from Florida Christmas Eve, and I want everything to be nice." Her bank account was precariously low, but she'd found so many things she knew her mother would like.

"How long is your mom staying?"

Lana bit her lip and studied the bent pliers. "I'm not sure. Mom is sort of...flexible. A couple of days, I'm guessing." Unless she was in a hurry to get back to Gary or Larry or whatever his name was...this week.

"She's welcome to my room. I'll be in Houston visiting my sister and her family for a few days."

She stood and dusted her backside. "Thanks, but she'll probably stay in my room, and I'll take the pullout."

"Well, at least I won't be underfoot." He smiled sheepishly and splayed his hands. "I don't normally sleep this late, but I guess I was exhausted from unpacking yesterday."

She gestured to the new furniture, stylishly situated amongst her own. "I'm sorry I didn't have a chance to help you."

"You're a lifesaver just to take me in on such short notice."

"That goes both ways."

"So—" he wagged his eyebrows "—how was your date last night? Or am I being too nosy?"

"You're not being too nosy," she said, her voice high and innocent. "But it wasn't a date. It was a business meeting." At the end of which, she and Greg had gotten half-naked on the bar. Business meetings at Ladd-Markham had been somewhat less...revealing. "Would you like some tea?"

He nodded and sat on one of the two red stools she'd dragged out of a Dumpster and repainted years ago. She poured them both a cup of tea with cream, then joined him at the counter.

"So, Lana, what's your story?"

She blew on the surface of her tea. "What do you mean?"

"You're a great-looking gal who owns her own business and, from what I can see, is pretty darn smart. Why hasn't some Kentucky stud tied you to his hitching post?"

She laughed. "Because this filly rather likes her freedom."

"You're not lonely?"

"No," she lied breezily.

"Says the woman who lives with a blow-up doll," he teased.

Lana glanced over at her plastic, grinning sidekick. "Harry's a gem, isn't he?"

"Where on earth did you find him?"

Her memories rewound, sliding past her. "I met Harry at a bachelorette party in college. The bride-to-be brought him and passed him off to a single friend, and the tradition continued. One day I got this box in the mail, and Harry was inside. Now he's mine."

"Until you're married?"

She grinned. "Well, that's the idea. But I think I've had him longer than anyone. Going on three years now."

"Is there anyone else left in the group who's single?"

Lana pursed her mouth and nodded. "A few, I think. There were these two sisters from Chicago. Seems like they're still single." She brightened. "But no matter—I plan to keep him around for quite a while. The shop requires so much attention, I don't have time for a man."

"Uh-oh."

"Uh-oh, what?"

"Uh-oh, that's when love always knocks you down—when it's least convenient."

She scoffed. "I'm firmly on my feet." Okay, Greg had had her on her back for a few seconds last night, but everyone was allowed one mistake. "So, Rich, what's *your* story?"

He shook his head. "It's not a bestseller."

"Try me."

After a gulp of tea, he shrugged. "Lots of failed relationships with women. I admitted about a year ago that I'm gay."

"And how's that going?" she asked mildly.

"Admitting I'm gay is one thing, but entering into a relationship is something else. I'm not ready."

But she recognized the longing in his voice. Loneliness had the same address regardless of a person's reasons for being there. She sighed. Was that why she'd clicked on a primal level with Greg Healey—was he also lonely?

Rich stood and walked to the window, then turned back with a broad smile. "But I have a good feeling about Lexington, Lana, like something significant is going to happen for me here."

She returned his smile. "Then it will." The man truly was handsome, she acknowledged. Handsome and...comfortable. She sighed. Why couldn't all relationships be like this? Sexual tension ruined everything by tying tongues, quickening tempers, sensitizing erogenous zones.

Lana sipped her tea. She wasn't looking forward to seeing Greg Healey again today. Really, she wasn't.

"What's his name?"

"Greg," she blurted, then realized her gaffe. "I mean, who?"

"The man you're not thinking about."

She frowned miserably. "Greg Healey."

"Nice name."

"*Not* a nice guy."

"So why bother?"

She could have said she'd been forced to work with him on the rezoning project, but councilwoman Wheeler had given her a choice. There was something about the man... She shook her head, at a loss. "I honestly don't know."

"Can I hazard a guess?"

Lana shrugged.

"You think that, deep down, everyone is good, and you like trying to tap into that goodness."

"What makes you think that?"

"From talking to you, from looking around your shop

and seeing the causes you care about. It's refreshing," he added quickly. "But it also sets you up for disappointment when people turn out to be...themselves. What does this guy do for a living?"

Her frown deepened. "He's an attorney."

Rich gasped and covered his mouth. "How dare he?"

She laughed. "I don't have anything against attorneys in general. It's just that *this* attorney seems to only want to use his power and money to get more power and more money."

"Sounds personal. You're not the least bit attracted to this guy?"

In the short time she'd known him, she'd observed Rich Enderling display uncanny insight into the people around him. The man missed nothing. The creamed tea curdled in her throat as it went down. "I think what I feel for Greg Healey is the morbid fascination one has with a person who can destroy one's life as one knows it. And for the record, I do take my livelihood personally."

"Maybe he truly believes the rezoning plan will be good for the city."

"Whose side are you on?"

He grinned. "Yours—because if you lose your job, you might lose this great apartment, and then where would I be?"

"At the Y."

"So all I'm saying is that I think you're right—that there's good in everybody. For some people, though, it takes a special person or the right circumstances to bring that goodness to the surface." He shrugged. "Who knows? You might be the person who brings out the best in Greg Healey."

She winced. "I haven't told you how he and I really met."

"Now I'm intrigued."

She glanced at her watch. "It's a long story, and I have to open the shop. How about lunch on me?"

"I never pass up a free meal or a good story. But then I have to drop off the U-Haul trailer."

"Okay. Just one more thing."

"Yeah?"

"Um, Greg Healey is working in the shop today."

He lifted an eyebrow.

"*Only* because I challenged him to get to know the business owners better before he rezones us all out of a job. So if he drops by while you're there, ip zay your ip lay."

Rich walked over to Harry and put his arm around the doll's shoulder. "Harry, man, it's been nice knowing you. But don't worry, the food's great in Chicago."

GREG DROVE AROUND the coffee shop three times looking for a parking place. Regret for his hasty response to Lana's challenge last night had built in his stomach since the minute he awoke this morning from a fitful sleep. He chewed on the inside of his cheek—he'd simply go in, dispense a few cups of coffee, and get out. Quick and painless; one hour, tops. And no way was he going to wear an apron.

The worst part had been trying to explain to Will why he was going to "work for Lana" today. He'd been tempted to lie, but lying to Will was difficult any day of the week, and impossible on Sunday while hanging outside Christmas lights. Watching his brother's childlike reaction to the twinkling decorations when they'd finished had reminded him that it was a good thing he'd fielded Lana's ad for his brother, or else Will would have fallen head over heels for the woman.

Greg pulled into a cramped parking spot and squeezed out the door. Blaming his accelerated heartbeat on the extra cup of coffee he'd needed to get going this morning, Greg pushed open the door to the shop.

His gaze went first to Lana, who looked long and lush in a straight, blue velvet jumper that fell to her ankles, and a white turtleneck. Nearly every inch of her was covered, but the image of her naked to the waist overrode the present. With much effort, his gaze next went to the man seated on a stool in front of her. Kissing Man.

Greg set his jaw. What the devil was *he* doing here?

They both turned in his direction, and Lana didn't even have the good grace to look sheepish. Instead, she offered up a guileless smile. "Hello there. I figured you'd changed your mind."

"No. Although I can't stay more than an hour or so."

She glanced at the clock, one of those bird clocks that were annoying as hell. "It'll get busy soon. Come on around, and I'll show you how things work."

He walked behind the bar, supremely self-conscious. Kissing Man watched him carefully.

"Rich Enderling," the guy said, thrusting his hand over the bar.

"Greg Healey," he said, returning a firm handshake.

"Rich is a friend of mine," Lana interjected, but she was talking fast and her voice was artificially high. "He was just leaving, weren't you, Rich?"

Rich seemed amused when he looked back to her. "Yeah. I'll see you tonight?"

She seemed exasperated. "Yes. Goodbye."

"Thanks for lunch." He glanced back to Greg. "Nice to meet you."

Greg gave him a curt nod.

Lana's gaze followed the man until he left, her movements suspended until the door closed behind him. Then her body relaxed, as if she'd just escaped some near miss. A chime sounded—the same noise that had interrupted them last night, seconds shy of making love. His body warmed, and from the color that bloomed in her cheeks, he assumed she was remembering, as well. "Excuse me," she said. "That'll be Andy from the soup kitchen."

"Soup kitchen?"

"I give them my day-old pastries."

Of course she did. "Let me give you a hand."

"No, the boxes are stacked by the door. I just need to let him in. If you get any customers, dazzle them for a few minutes with brilliant conversation."

The swing of her hips as she hurried away sent a spasm of lust surging to his midsection. Greg gripped the counter, cursing his curious weakness where she was concerned. Thankfully, the bell on the front door rang, announcing a customer. Feeling a little foolish, Greg prepared to stall the person, until he realized it was Rich Enderling returning.

"Lana's in the back," Greg said with a jerk of his head.

"Would you let her know that I'll cook dinner this evening when I get home?"

Greg blinked. "Home?"

The man nodded.

His stomach knotted. "You two *live* together?"

He nodded again. "I moved in last night. She's a real catch, isn't she? See you around, Craig."

The man gave him a triumphant little salute, then exited with a spring in his step. Greg scowled after him and muttered, "That's *Greg*."

LANA WAVED GOODBYE to Andy, then paused a moment to calm the beating of her heart. Good grief, after his humiliating near accusation last night that she had men all over the place, she had hoped to be appropriately irritated with him this morning, or at least indifferent. Instead she had a weird tingling, breathless sensation that she didn't want him to leave the room.

Holy hormones, what was wrong with her?

She inhaled and exhaled deeply, then reminded herself that this little "shadow" exercise today was to make Greg feel invested in the area. Too many people were counting on her for her to let herself be distracted by last night's misguided encounter. So she pasted on a professional smile and returned to the front of the shop, steeling herself against him.

Greg was standing with his back to her, leaning one hand on the bar, looking out the window as if he wanted to be anywhere but here. Dark slacks hugged slim, muscular hips she recognized as part of a runner's physique. A sparkling white collarless dress shirt spanned his broad shoulders—shoulders that bowed slightly as though under the pressure of something. Was it this rezoning project? Personal demons? She couldn't guess because the man was so unreachable. Last night she'd thought he'd relaxed a tiny bit on the ride over from the restaurant. She might even have ventured to say they had fun. But today...well, after last night...

Perfectly creased and starched—indeed, Greg looked as if he belonged anywhere but here. The differences in their lifestyles and their futures couldn't have been more apparent.

"I have an apron with your name on it," she said with forced cheer.

He turned, and she blinked at the dark look on his face. "I'll pass on the apron if it's all the same to you."

She shrugged, wondering why the man didn't have whiplash from his sudden mood swings. "Then I guess the Santa hat is out of the question."

He frowned more deeply.

She tried to laugh. "That sour face of yours will scare off my customers."

"I'm not much of a people person."

"Really? I wouldn't have guessed."

"Your roommate came back."

She couldn't hide her surprise or her alarm. Rich suspected she was developing feelings for Greg. Had he said something? "Wh-what did Rich want?"

"He said he'd fix dinner this evening."

"Is that all?"

He nodded, then gestured to the bar and laughed awkwardly. "Look, this was a bad idea."

"Then why did you agree to do it?"

His mouth tightened and his gaze pierced her. "I wasn't thinking straight last night."

She swallowed. "That makes two of us."

He ran his hand down over his face. "The sooner we hash through this rezoning plan, the sooner we can get back to our own lives."

"You mean the sooner we can forget we ever met?"

He shrugged, and his nonchalance squeezed her heart painfully. She hadn't realized how much she had hoped... That rich and powerful Greg Healey would fall so hopelessly in love with her that he would change his whole outlook on life? For a woman with an above-average IQ, she could be so dim.

"You're right," she managed to say. "Why don't I see if someone can cover for me today, so you and I can take a walk around the Parkland area and meet some of the other shop owners?"

"Whatever speeds things along," he said in an uninterested voice.

Fighting an ache of frustration, Lana called Wesley first, then Annette. Annette's ankle was better, and she agreed to come in as soon as possible. In the meantime, Lana showed Greg how to work the coffee dispensers. Supremely out of his element, he moved stiffly with a frown pulling at his face. Last night's encounter hung in the air around him, like a song she couldn't put out of her head, compromising her focus.

He seemed as cagey as she, reluctant to draw closer than an arm's length lest whatever had come over them last night strike again. But the space behind the bar was tight, and, truthfully, he was in the way more than he helped. She was constantly brushing past him, reaching behind him, or stepping around him, every movement bolstering her throbbing awareness of his body in close proximity to hers.

In her rush to wait on an impatient customer, Lana tripped over Greg's feet and fell into him. He steadied her, but not before hot coffee sloshed over the cup she was holding and down the front of his pristine white shirt. He gasped and held the fabric away from him, leaving her with the bad feeling he'd have a third-degree burn in the shape of his undershirt.

"I'm so sorry," she murmured, dabbing at the runaway stain halfheartedly. The shirt was ruined—and she doubted that he'd bought it on a clearance table.

"You burned your hand," he said, then pulled her to the sink and ran cold water over the pink tingling flesh.

"It's nothing," she protested, but admitted the water felt good on her scorched palm. Or was it his fingers on her hand, brown skin against white, that felt good? He stood just behind her, his head bent close to hers. Perhaps the hot coffee had stirred up his cologne, because the musky scent enveloped her, teasing her senses, dredging up a flood of forgotten sensations from last night. She was grateful he couldn't see that her face was as pink as her injured hand. Had the oxygen in the air suddenly decreased?

"Thanks, it's better," she said, then pulled her shaky hand from his and dried it on her apron.

He unbuttoned the top couple of buttons on his stained shirt to expose his throat and collarbone to the air, and her cheeks burned with the realization that she knew the planes of the rest of his torso in intimate detail.

"The first rule of working in a coffee shop," she said with a rueful laugh, "is not to wear white."

"I guess I should've taken the apron," he said, then one side of his mouth pulled back. "But at least now my shirt matches my torn jacket."

Lana winced. "I haven't had a chance to get your jacket repaired yet."

"Can I get some service here?" a man asked loudly from the other side of the bar.

She opened her mouth to apologize, but Greg spoke first. "Take it easy, man. Can't you see the lady burned her hand?"

"All I see is you making moon eyes at her," the customer said dryly. "Can I have my coffee, or what?"

Greg's face was a thundercloud, so Lana cut in and handled the man's order, her mind humming like a teenager's at the offhand comment. Had Greg been making moon eyes at her? Nah. More likely, his eyes had been dilated in pain from his scalding hot coffee bath. She busied herself filling orders, until, as was the way of retail, the customers were gone and a lull ensued. Lana glanced at her watch. Where the devil was Annette?

Greg wore a closed expression, and he, too, checked the time. He had better things to do, of course. But at least business had been good for the short time he'd been there. Maybe he would realize that she provided a service that people wanted. That he couldn't just go around uprooting people's lives, like he'd uprooted hers.

At a loss for conversation, she gestured to a nearby table with a game board. "Do you play chess?"

He shrugged. "It's been a while."

"Come on, I'll go easy on you."

But he snorted softly as he sat down. "I'm a pretty good player."

So he'd belonged to the science club *and* the chess club. "Well, I'm not so bad myself."

He cracked his knuckles in a sweeping motion. "Give it your best shot."

She looked into his dark eyes, and for a split second she wondered if he were talking about the game, or about trying to breach his stony exterior. He looked away and gravely set up the game pieces. The tiniest of smug smiles played on his lips, and Lana shook her head. *The bigger they are, the harder they fall.*

Six moves later she announced, "Checkmate."

"Huh?" Greg jammed his hand into his hair as he stared down at the chessboard. "That's impossible. We've barely moved any pieces."

Instead of scoffing at his disbelief, she swallowed hard at the sudden realization that his large, handsome features were becoming too familiar, and too appealing. She pushed back her chair—she needed some distance. "While you're second-guessing me, I'm going to sort the recyclables." She grabbed a couple of paper cups from a table as she walked by, then slipped behind the bar, trying to keep her gaze from straying to him. She needed to get a grip.

"How did you do that?" he asked, gesturing to the game board.

"Diversion," she said. "While you were pursuing my queen, you left your king at risk."

His head was still bent, and his index finger moved, re-creating plays in his head.

"Can you handle refills for about five minutes?" she asked.

He waved and frowned, which she interpreted as yes.

Fighting a smile, Lana wheeled the garbage down the hall to where the recycle bins were stacked behind a folding door. She separated paper, glass, plastic.

Undoubtedly, no one had ever beat Greg Healey at chess, and certainly not a complicated female-type. *Paper, glass, plastic.* Most likely, the women he met through the singles ads had more lively pursuits. *Paper, glass, plastic.* She closed the folding door with a sigh and headed back to the front.

Lana froze at the sight of her smiling pastry chef Annette coming through the front door. Good grief, she'd forgotten. The last thing she needed was for Annette to reveal that *she* was Coffee Girl and fall head over heels in love with Greg Healey. He'd trample the woman's heart for sure. And Lana should know.

Lana blinked with the revelation, then shouted "Annette!" before the girl's hand left the doorknob. Lana glided past Greg, who had moved behind the bar. "Thanks for coming in."

Annette cast a quizzical glance toward Greg, who was, amazingly, wiping up the counter. "Who's that?"

Lana lowered her voice conspiratorially. "Um, he's the owner of the building, the one who's trying to rezone the area and close me down."

Annette pursed her lips. "Close you down? Looks to me like he's cleaning up."

Lana rolled her eyes for effect. "He's only here to prove to the city council that he's concerned about the merchants."

"He's gorgeous. What's his name?"

She took in Annette's perky face and voluptuous figure, and suddenly realized that keeping Annette and Greg apart had little to do with her concern for Annette's fragile heart. Was it possible that she wanted to keep him all to herself? Preposterous, considering the man probably answered singles ads every week. Still...

Her heart skipped a beat in relief when she remembered that Annette didn't know the last name of the man who had answered her ad. "It's, um, Mr. Healey. Listen, Annette, while you're here, I wondered if you could do me a little favor." Lana led a craning Annette past the bar out of sight to a coat closet in the back. She withdrew Greg's torn jacket. "Is it possible to repair this tear so that it doesn't show?"

Annette studied the rip. "Nice fabric. Whose jacket?"

"Um, the guy out front."

She grinned. "What did you do? Tear his clothes off in a fight?"

"Can you fix it or not?"

Annette nodded. "To the point that it won't be noticeable."

Lana sighed with relief. At least she wouldn't have to replace an expensive suit on her already strained budget. "Great. Write me up a bill when you're finished."

"No charge. It's the least I can do for accidentally setting you up with that creepy Greg What's-his-name last week."

"Shh!"

"What?"

"I thought I heard something."

"I didn't hear anything."

Lana waved off the imaginary noise. "Thanks for watching the shop for me."

"With that hunky guy? No problem."

Lana frowned. "Actually, I was planning to take Hunky Guy around to meet some of the other shop owners that he wants to put out of business."

Annette's face fell. "Oh."

Lana untied her apron and handed it to Annette. "I'll be back soon."

"Take your time," Annette said, winking. "Maybe you can sweet-talk Mr. Healey into not going through with his plan." She laughed. "And if he doesn't cooperate, you can always spray his eyes full of hair spray like you did that other guy."

LANA DROVE HER HANDS deeper into her coat pockets and glanced sideways at Greg. "Now that you've met some of the shop owners, what do you think?" Her shop was in sight, up ahead and on the opposite side of the street. The weather had taken a sudden turn toward raw, spitting ice crystals and blowing up sudden blasts of Arctic wind. She could no longer feel her toes or her nose, but, curiously, she hated for the tour to end.

"Not the friendliest bunch," he said wryly.

"You're trying to shut down their businesses."

"How many times do I have to tell you that this isn't personal—it's business?"

She stopped and turned to face him. "It's personal to me."

He stopped, too, and a muscle ticked in his jaw. He'd turned up the collar of his sleek black leather coat to ward off the biting wind. "You shouldn't allow personal entanglements to cloud your business judgment."

"I can't make decisions without considering the people who will be affected," she said softly. "I'm not wired that way."

He looked away, jammed his hands into this pockets, then looked back. "I'm not responsible for those people. If their livelihoods are tied up in their businesses, why haven't any of them offered to buy their buildings?"

"Because they can't afford them?" She knew *she* couldn't afford a mortgage on the building her shop was in.

"That's right," he said. "They can't afford to carry a mortgage and pay the property taxes and maintain the rotten plumbing. They want to have a say-so in how the property is developed, but none of them are rushing to assume the risk."

He was right, of course. At least in her case. "Last night you said you would help."

"Last night I was...distracted." Regret laced his words.

Her heart shivered with disappointment. "Meaning, you would have said anything to get in my pants?"

He shook his head and rubbed his jaw. "Don't put words in my mouth. I said I would *try* to help, and I will, but there's more at stake here than a few miscellaneous shops. Look, I have to go. I've wasted—" He stopped and scratched his temple to cover his gaffe, but she'd heard him loud and clear. He'd wasted enough time on her.

"I have to go," he said simply.

She struggled to keep the hurt from her voice, angry at herself because she had no right to feel hurt. Greg Healey meant nothing to her. She reached into her shoulder bag and withdrew a folder of photocopied notes—all her scribbled thoughts for regenerating the Hyde Parkland area. "For what it's worth, these are my ideas," she said, thrusting the folder into his hand. "I'll see you around."

Lana crossed the street and walked toward the shop. It was a good thing she knew the route by heart, or else she'd never have found the place through the blur of tears—caused by the stinging wind, of course.

17

"GREGORY?"

Greg snapped out of another Lana-induced reverie. "What?"

"Do you think that Eddie Age Seven would like the red bike helmet or the blue?"

"The blue."

Will grinned. "I think so, too." He added the box to a toy-laden buggy. "That's the last one on the list. This is fun."

"Thanks for coming to help me, pal." The past week had been a blur of disjointed events. He'd left things badly with Lana, and his regret had escalated each day. Her folder of notes had become his bedtime reading, which dovetailed perfectly into dreaming about the woman. Greg dragged his hand down his face. He was feeling a little stressed.

"How do we get the gifts to the boys and girls?"

"We'll take them back to the coffee shop, and Lana will make sure they go to the right person." Of course, his dilemma was how to get the gifts to Lana's coffee shop without running into her. He'd considered posting them, but with only five more mailing days until Christmas, he was afraid the packages would be waylaid.

"I'm sorry that you and Lana had an argument."

He frowned. "How did you know we had an argument?"

"I heard you telling Yvonne."

"Oh. Well, it wasn't an argument—it was a disagreement."

"But Yvonne said you were the disagreeable one."

"It's not nice to eavesdrop on other people's conversations."

"But I thought you were trying to be nice to Lana to win her over to your side."

He sighed. "It's complicated."

"I know you said that women are complicated, Gregory, but I still want one."

Oh, no, not that again. "You're not looking in the singles ads again, are you?"

"Nope. Coffee Girl was the only one I liked, but she turned out to be complicated, too, didn't she."

Greg's head was spinning, but he managed a nod.

"I guess I'll just have to wait until the right girl comes along." Will lifted a fire truck from the buggy and moved the ladder up and down. "Lana's a good person, isn't she, Gregory?"

"Do we have to talk about Lana?"

"Well, she is a nice person, isn't she?"

He swallowed hard. "I suppose." He could always have the gifts couriered over.

"So why are you shutting down her coffee shop?"

"Will, we've been over this a dozen times." But what the heck was he so afraid of? He would just drive over there and drop them off. Period.

"I know, Gregory, but I don't understand why everybody can't be happy."

He massaged the bridge of his nose. "It's impossible for everybody to be happy at the same time." He would simply park, and let Will take the packages inside.

"I want to buy Yvonne a suitcase for Christmas."

He sighed in relief at Will's sudden diversion. "I think

that's a very good idea. Why don't you go to the luggage department, and I'll—"

"Mr. Healey?"

Greg turned to see Lana's friend Alex walking toward him. He wasn't sure how to respond. The woman hadn't exactly been friendly when he'd met her, although now she looked cordial enough. "Hello," he said. "I know Tremont's is your family's store, but I didn't expect you to be here all the time."

"Christmas shopping with a friend, same as you," she said, then glanced over his shoulder. "Here's my friend now."

Greg turned his head and stemmed a groan as councilwoman Wheeler walked up with a smug smile. "Mr. Healey, what a surprise."

"Ms. Wheeler." He looked back and forth between the women. "Somehow I'm not quite as surprised as you are." He introduced Will to both women.

"I saw you at the council meeting," Alex said to Will.

"You mean the meeting where Gregory was trying to shut down Lana's coffee shop?"

"*Will.*" Greg forced a laugh and clapped his brother on the back. "We've been over this."

The councilwoman offered up a little smile. "I've tried to reach you every day this week."

He'd played hooky every day this week, taking up residence in the back row of the city courthouse, even renewing old acquaintanceships with law buddies he ran into in the halls. His secretary was ready to quit. "I was going to return your call first thing in the morning." A lie.

She nodded. "And how are things going between you and Ms. Martina?"

"Fine," he said with as much enthusiasm as he could summon.

"They had a big argument," Will supplied.

"A little disagreement." Greg shot Will a warning look.

"Oh? Do I need to intervene?" the councilwoman asked, her tone a subtle threat.

"No," he assured her. "In fact, I'll be seeing Ms. Martina today." Two lies in two minutes.

"Gregory bought all these toys for Lana's children."

"For needy children that Lana sponsors," Greg clarified.

Both women arched an eyebrow, and he wondered if his face was as red as it felt.

"That's generous of you, Mr. Healey," the councilwoman said.

"*Very* generous," Alex seconded.

He shifted uncomfortably. No one had ever called him *generous*. "Well, it was nice seeing both of you."

"I look forward to that call in the morning, Mr. Healey, with an update on the progress you've made."

He managed a shaky smile. "Absolutely."

LANA SLIPPED THE BUSINESS CARD Greg had given her the night of the council meeting out of her apron pocket and studied it again, as if somewhere between the lines of formal raised script announcing, "Gregory K. Healey, President and Chief Legal Counsel, Healey Land Group," she would find some encrypted code to reinforce her suspicion that Greg Healey, Science Club guy, lurked just beneath the surface and was someone worth knowing.

The edges of the card were rounded from her constant fingering over the past week. She regretted walking away from him in anger last Sunday because no matter how the man affected her, the shop owners were counting on her to work out a compromise. She had to find a way to overcome their personal...difficulties, and break through his mind-set that newer was better.

She'd called him at work every day the past week, but hadn't identified herself or left a message when his secretary said he was out of the office. Out of the office for an entire week? Greg didn't strike her as the kind of man who vacationed frivolously, so perhaps he'd been traveling. Regardless, after a week of no contact, she was starting to panic because the days before the final council vote were slipping away.

Calling him at home was out of the question if they were going to maintain a professional relationship. She would phone him again in the morning and leave her name if he wasn't available. And if he hadn't returned her call by midweek, she would be forced to call councilwoman Wheeler and ask her to intervene—a thought that made Lana ill. If Greg told Wheeler why they couldn't work together, her credibility would be ruined.

And with good reason, she noted miserably. The merchants had trusted her when they'd asked her to be their spokesperson, and she might have compromised their position by succumbing to the physical attraction she felt for Greg. She groaned aloud and dropped her head into her hands. How had her life gone downhill so quickly? The respite of her mother's Christmas Eve visit loomed like an emotional gift. Janet was nothing if not entertaining.

The bell on the back door rang, and Lana dragged herself up to answer it, surprised to find Annette holding a covered tray emitting a wonderful aroma.

"I hope it's chocolate," Lana said.

Annette cringed. "Bad day?"

"Crummy."

"It's a new recipe—chocolate pound cake."

"I love you." She held the door open for Annette to squeeze by. "Not that I'm not glad to see you, but what are you doing here?"

"You seemed kind of blue this week, so I thought I'd drop off these goodies and try to cheer you up."

She smiled and followed Annette to the pastry case. "You're a dear. Have you had any more responses to your ad?"

"One extremely humiliating fraternity prank, one guy who just got out of Attica, and one guy who was about a hundred years old."

"Ouch."

"I know. So as appalling as Greg What's-his-face was to you, he's still the best thing that came out of that stupid ad."

Lana squirmed. "Well, the holidays are the worst time to start a new relationship. You'll probably get some takers after the first of the year."

"I hope so." They crouched behind the pastry case and used tongs to arrange the slices of dark moist cake that smelled like heaven.

"You'll meet Mr. Right soon," Lana said, although she was feeling a little down on love these days.

Not that she was in love with Greg. Or anything like that.

Annette laughed ruefully. "I hope so. But I have to admit I'm getting a little discouraged. Why can't the man of my dreams just walk through the door?"

The bell on the front door rang, sending them into a fit of giggles. But when Lana straightened to see Greg and Will, their arms laden with Christmas packages, she sobered with a hiccup.

"Hi, Lana," Will said with a grin. "Gregory and I bought presents for your kids."

She frowned. "My kids?" Then she remembered the needy-children Christmas tree, picked clean of name tags. "My kids!" Her gaze flew to Greg. "*You* took all the tags?" Slow wonder crept into her heart.

"It's no big deal," he said casually. "I wouldn't want to start a rumor that I'm a nice guy." But his faint blush belied his nonchalance.

Telling herself not to overreact, Lana pressed her lips together to suppress her happiness at seeing him again and to hide how much his gesture had touched her. "No, we wouldn't want to start a nasty rumor like that."

He shifted the load in his arms. "We put the gifts in bags so you can double-check everything."

She nodded, unable to tear her gaze from his. "You can put the gifts under the tree if you like."

He stared back, and once again she caught a glimpse of the man beneath the stoic facade before he looked away. "Come on, Will, we still have more packages to unload from the car—Will?"

Will's eyes were wide and riveted on some point behind her shoulder. Lana turned to see a similar expression on Annette's face as she peeked over the top of the pastry case. A slow smile crept up Lana's face. "Will, this is my pastry chef, Annette Bowman. Annette, this is William Healey."

"You can call me Will," he blurted.

"Hello, Will," she murmured.

Time stood still as the unmistakable instant attraction reverberated between them. Lana had the distinct feeling that she was witnessing the birth of something special, and for a split second, she was envious of Annette's good fortune. She sighed, then chanced a glance at Greg, who seemed less sure of what was happening.

"Will? Are you going to help me with the packages?"

"I'll help," Annette announced, then moved in slow motion from behind the counter to stand in front of Will.

"Do you have a boyfriend?" he asked.

Lana bit back a smile at his forthrightness.

Annette shook her head no, sending her red curls bouncing.

"Will you go to a Christmas party with me Friday night?"

She nodded yes, sending her curls bouncing in the other direction, then took the packages from Greg's arms and led Will toward the stage where the Christmas trees sat with packages scattered beneath.

Greg stared after them, then looked at Lana. "What just happened?"

"I think your brother just asked my friend out on a date."

He frowned suspiciously. "What sort of girl is she?"

Lana crossed her arms. "The sort of girl your brother likes, apparently."

"He doesn't know about these things."

"And you do?"

Greg's first impulse was to say that yes, he did. He knew that women were high-maintenance, emotional creatures who complicated the simplest of issues. He knew a woman would drive a wedge between him and his brother. He knew a woman said one thing when she meant something else entirely. But as always, Lana's eyes derailed his thoughts. "Huh?"

"And you do know about these things?"

He dragged his gaze and thoughts back to Will. "This isn't about me."

"They're only going to a party, for heaven's sake."

At least he would be able to keep an eye on them. And beforehand he would sit down with Will and make sure he understood how risky it was to have unprotected sex. His brother had good intentions about waiting until he was married, but in the heat of the moment, sometimes good intentions went out the window. Greg frowned. No one knew that better than he.

This Annette person was cute, no doubt. Oh, not *his* type at all—he definitely preferred tall women, and a more slender build. And the eyes...well, the eyes were important.

"Greg?"

Jarred from his thoughts by the voice he could not evict from his brain, he looked at Lana. "What?"

Her little frown told him she'd been trying to get his attention.

"I was saying that I feel bad about the way we left things last week. I was unprofessional, and I apologize—"

God, she had the most incredible eyes. And a slender figure. And she was tall.

"—And I was hoping," she continued, "that we could pick up where we left off."

And now he was confused about which came first—the definition of what kind of woman was his type or Lana Martina?

"Where we left off on the rezoning project," she added quickly.

He'd be able to keep an eye on Will most of the time Friday night, but if he had a date, they could double. Then he could check out this girl who had captured his brother's fancy. "Are you busy Friday night?" he asked Lana.

"I can get away."

"Then come to a party with me."

"A party?"

"Company function," he explained. "You can meet some of the folks who've been involved in the rezoning project from the beginning."

"It's business?" she asked, her voice wary.

"Strictly," he assured her.

"Okay. What time and where?"

"We'll pick you up."

"We?"

He gestured across the room. "Will and Annette and I. We'll all go together."

18

LANA'S LINGERING QUESTIONS about why she had agreed to go to the party with Greg were banished when she opened the door to her apartment. Frustrating or not, she missed his company. His eyes widened at the sight of her in the long black sheath with spaghetti straps that dated back to Ladd-Markham cocktail parties.

"Wow," he murmured.

Ridiculously pleased, she said, "Wow yourself," surveying his immaculate charcoal-gray suit, blinding white shirt and deep red tie. The colors suited him immensely. "Come in while I get my wrap."

He strolled in warily, and she suspected he was remembering the last time he'd visited her apartment. The man's eyes were probably watering.

"Is your roomie home?" he asked.

"No," she called over her shoulder. "Rich is working late." In her bedroom, she checked her carefully applied makeup one more time, then adjusted the rhinestone barrettes scattered through the layers of her hair. Satisfied that she looked festive, she retrieved her shoulder wrap from the foot of the bed, breathed deeply to slow her pulse, then returned to the living room.

"I see you still have Harry," he said with a wry smile.

"Oh, I'll always have Harry." As fond as she was of Harry, the past few days she'd begun to see him as a symbol of always being alone. She liked her own company, but she also held out hope that someday she'd meet someone to share her life with.

Such as it was. If her life could so easily be set on end, maybe she wasn't living the existence of substance she had haughtily assumed. Pressing her lips together in thought, she draped the wrap over one shoulder, then twisted to reach behind her.

"Allow me," Greg murmured near her ear, then he lifted the other end of the wrap and placed it around her shoulders.

Her breath caught in her chest as his hand lingered longer than necessary upon the sensitive hollow of her collarbone. Their date was strictly business, he'd said—and she needed to keep her wits about her. But her body had its own agenda, established when his warm breath tickled the nape of her neck. She closed her eyes against the onslaught of desire, holding herself rigid to suppress the urge to lean back into his body.

"Please, Greg."

His breath grew warmer and more rapid upon her neck, although he fell short of lowering his lips to her skin.

"Please, what?" he whispered, his voice heavy with the promise of fulfillment.

Her breasts tightened, the peaks hardening at the memory of his silky mouth, but she turned her head away from him. "Please...let's go."

"Right," he said, clearing his voice. "Sorry."

She turned to face him, drawing the wrap over her tingling breasts. "Greg, I'd be a fool not to notice this... attraction between us, but things are already complicated enough."

"Complicated," he said, shoving his hands into his pockets. "That they are."

"If only..." Lana bit her tongue. If only they'd met at a

bar somewhere instead of through a missed connection in the classified ads. If only he didn't own the building where her shop was located... "Never mind, let's go." Quashing the memory of his touch, she retrieved her evening purse and door key.

He held open the door for her, but his strained expression indicated he was still struggling with the effects of their brush with intimacy.

"I would say that Will and Annette are wondering what's keeping us, but they don't seem to realize that anything else is going on in the world."

She locked the door and smiled. "That's sweet. Annette told me they've talked on the phone every night this week. She adores him."

"Maybe for now," Greg said. "But how long will that last?"

Lana glanced up sharply as they descended the stairs. "You're not giving your brother much credit."

"I didn't mean it that way," he said. "I just know..."

"You just know what?"

"I just know how women are."

She lifted an eyebrow. "Oh? And how are we?"

One side of his mouth drew back. "I don't want Will to get hurt."

"You don't know Annette—she's a good person. She would never lead Will on."

"Will wouldn't need much encouragement. He's still, um, innocent in some areas."

She laughed softly as they approached the big Mercedes. "You have nothing to worry about where Annette is concerned. She's the original little Miss Innocent."

Greg frowned toward the car. "If she's the original little Miss Innocent, then why are the windows fogged up?"

She followed his gaze, then winced and picked up her

pace to match his. "It's cold, they're probably running the heater."

"That's one way to put it," he said dryly. He strode to the car and rapped on the front passenger window before opening the door for her.

The inside light came on, illuminating the couple in the back seat tangled in an embrace. They pulled apart and turned wide eyes toward the intruders. Lana swallowed a smile at the sight of Annette's red lipstick transferred to Will's face.

"Hi, Gregory. Hi, Lana."

Lana looked at Greg and discreetly covered her mouth to keep from bursting out laughing. He, on the other hand, did not look amused. "Hello, Will." Lana allowed Greg to help her into the seat, then flinched when he banged the door shut. Through the condensation on the window, she watched him stalk around the front of the car. Lana chuckled to herself. The man would be a force to reckon with if he ever had a daughter.

The unbidden thought sent an odd sensation to her stomach. What on earth made her picture him in a domestic situation? Of all the men she'd met, Greg Healey was probably the man least likely to make a trip down the aisle. He wore his bachelorhood like a sign on his sleeve: Do Not Enter.

He opened the driver's door and swung inside. A sigh passed over his lips, then he removed a snowy handkerchief and handed it over his shoulder. "Wipe your face, man," he said quietly.

"Okay, Gregory."

The gentle exchange brought unexpected tears to her eyes, and for the first time she had a glimpse into why Greg seemed old for his years. Did his responsibility for Will fuel his ambition and explain why he was such a seriously confirmed bachelor? In that moment his stoic personality seemed endearing, and his pursuits, noble. While he facilitated large real estate transactions every day, she was selling half-caf-nonfat-whip-extra-mochas. In the scheme of things, her contribution to society seemed pretty darn trivial, a concept she'd given a lot of thought to this week. Greg's secretary had called her several times to clarify Lana's notes as she was typing them up, so at least he hadn't discarded the ideas she'd given him.

But as they drove through the Hyde Parkland area, Lana saw every empty building, every overgrown lot, every graffitied bus stop, as if she were seeing it all for the first time. What had a week ago seemed like vintage charm, now smacked of urban neglect. Maybe Greg was right. Maybe the area needed renovation and a parking garage more than it needed a coffee shop.

She studied Greg's profile with grudging respect. She'd been little more than a thorn in his side since they met, yet he had taken the step to repair the lines of communication last Sunday when he and Will had come into the shop. A curious little quiver of revelation bloomed in her breast, stealing her breath. She was overwhelmed with the urge to touch him, to spend time with him, even if they were arguing. As crazy as her life had been the past couple of weeks, she'd never felt more alive. Was it possible to be in love with someone she barely knew?

Kissing noises sounded from the back seat. Maybe *so*, she conceded wryly. With Will and Annette, it had been love at first sight—ironic since it was Greg who had answered Annette's ad. Considering the way things had turned out, though, she was planning to keep that tidbit to herself.

Lana shook her head. Falling in love with Greg Healey— how dumb could she be? Not only was he one of the most unavailable men in the city, but their goals were so different. Even if the man were looking for a significant other—which he wasn't—a relationship between them would never work. Had she inherited her mother's knack for gravitating to men who were wrong for her? Lana chanced a glance sideways, wondering how hard Greg Healey would laugh if he could read her mind right now.

GREG WOULD HAVE GIVEN anything to be able to read Lana's mind. She'd been uncharacteristically quiet during their ride, forcing Greg to turn up the stereo to drown out the enthusiastic kissing in the back seat. And while his concern for Will remained uppermost in his mind, another concern had been gaining momentum over the past few days: his overwhelming attraction to Lana Martina. He didn't know what to make of this woman who had walked away from a lucrative field to become a struggling entrepreneur. Who sold coffee but drank tea, and played chess like a genius. Who volunteered time, space and resources to causes he merely read about in the Sunday paper. He glanced at her profile with new respect. Despite her quirks, Lana seemed to be a person of principle.

Greg pulled at his too-tight collar. Between their near miss at her apartment, and Will making out in the back seat like a teenager, Greg was no longer in the mood to go to the Christmas party.

Two weeks ago Art had called with what had seemed like the best news of his life. How had things deteriorated so rapidly?

When they walked into the small ballroom of the hotel, every person in the room craned for a look at Lana. Unreasonable pride swelled in Greg's chest. She *was* magnificent in that long, clingy black dress, and tonight she was on his arm. He'd always felt out of place at the company get-togethers because he'd always felt out of place at the helm of his father's company. But while he retrieved a glass of wine for each of them, he watched as Lana made the rounds, shaking hands and charming his employees, and was struck by the difference one person could make in a roomful of people...or in an organization.

Art Payton walked up to him, holding a hefty drink. "Who's the filly?"

Greg frowned. "Her name is Lana Martina. She owns a coffee shop in the building we have designated as a parking garage in the Hyde Parkland parcel."

Art nodded. "Best Cuppa Joe."

"You know the place?"

"Used to hang out there when I was single, about a hundred years ago."

He sighed. "Art, I've been thinking that maybe we should try to save some of the buildings down there, after all—you know, in the spirit of preservation."

Art's eyes narrowed. "You're not serious."

"Just thinking about it. Can you run some numbers for me?"

"I don't have to. If you start changing that parcel now, you're liable to spook all the developers, which means a big goose egg." Art elbowed him in the ribs and nodded to Lana. "And the spirit that's moving you, son, has nothing to do with preservation."

Greg frowned. "Just run the numbers."

He carried their wineglasses across the room and stopped where Lana was chatting with a knot of employees that included Peg. "They were out of cranberry juice. Is chardonnay okay?"

She gave him a heart-stalling smile. "Sure. Thank you."

He was vaguely aware that his employees were staring at him—especially his secretary. "Is something wrong, Peg?"

"Um, no, sir. The time off you took last week agrees with you, sir. You look...different."

Her words registered, but Greg couldn't take his eyes off Lana. She was a good conversationalist, and a natural people person. She was telling a humorous story that had everyone riveted, him included. When she finished, she launched into another topic of conversation. She held court for nearly an hour. Greg watched her unobtrusively while he walked the perimeter of the ballroom, shaking hands. His mood was buoyant tonight and he felt pretty certain it was because of Lana.

"I thought you weren't bringing a date, sir," Peg whispered at one point in the evening.

"She isn't a date," he murmured back. "We're working together on a project—you know that."

"Ms. Martina is beautiful, sir."

He looked at the owlish woman, noticing for the first time that she was wearing makeup. And did she always wear her hair like that? "Peg, why do you punctuate almost every sentence with 'sir'?"

She blinked. "Because, sir—I mean, because, um...it just seems right."

"But you called my father by his first name."

She fidgeted with her purse. "But your father, sir—I mean, your father, well, he was...friendly."

"Friendly?"

"You know, a nice man. Sir."

Her words knifed through him. "Nice?"

"Yes, sir. Nice."

Greg glanced around the room at the faces of the people who worked for him. He knew very few of them by their first names, and he knew nothing about their families, their hobbies, their concerns. They stood more than an arm's length from him when they spoke, and looked downright uncomfortable when he approached. The truth of Peg's comparison hit him hard. He wasn't a nice guy. Not like his father, not like Will.

Will.

His immediate concerns were put on hold when he realized he hadn't seen Will and his date for some time. "Peg, have you seen Will?"

"He left, sir."

Greg swallowed hard. "What?"

"I heard him tell Ms. Martina that he was taking a taxi home, sir."

To have sex, he thought instantly. Right now, Will and that Annette person were having sex in Will's bed. She'd be pregnant, and Will would insist on marrying her. Greg strode to Lana's side and pulled her away from the crowd. "We have to go."

"What's wrong?"

"Why didn't you tell me that Will and Annette left?"

She shrugged. "They were bored, so they went to your house."

"To do what?"

She frowned. "Probably to be alone."

He took her empty wineglass and handed it to a passing waiter. "Let's go."

"Where?"

"To my house. Yvonne is away visiting, and they can't be alone."

"Greg, they're consenting adults. Besides, I don't think they're going to do anything."

"You saw them in the car!"

"They were *kissing*, for heaven's sake."

"I'm going home to check on them. Are you coming with me or not?"

She sighed. "Only to keep you from doing something you'll regret."

19

"IT'S BEAUTIFUL," Lana murmured, as they made their way up a lighted stone walkway. Actually, "beautiful" was an understated adjective for the limestone mansion. Holy hotel. "Did you grow up here?"

He nodded absently, scanning the lighted windows, oblivious to her awe. "They've definitely been here." He unlocked the door and swung it open, then gestured for her to precede him.

"Just for the record, I don't think this is a good idea," she said as she walked into a foyer large enough to host a dinner party.

He closed the door, his head cocked for sound—but only silence greeted them. Thank goodness. She had visions of him crashing in on Will and Annette in an intimate embrace.

"Will?" he called, but there was no answer. He dropped his keys on a table in the hall and walked straight ahead, past a sweeping staircase and toward a lighted room. Lana followed, ogling the gray-and-pink marble tile laid down in a checkerboard pattern. She glimpsed a monstrous living room on one side, a gigantic dining room on the other. She felt like Alice in Wonderland, shrunk to miniature.

Their footsteps clicked against the smooth tile as they entered a gargantuan kitchen with *two* refrigerators, commercial grade. Enough storage for a couple of hundred cartons of Betty Crocker cake icing, at least.

"He left a note," he said, his voice tense as he snatched the piece of paper propped up on a cherry sideboard.

She turned in place, taking in the elegant glass-fronted cabinets, the solid-surface counters. Not a beanbag chair or a refurbished stool from the Dumpster in sight. "What does the note say?"

"They went to the stables where he works, to see the horses." Relief threaded his voice, and he sagged against the counter.

"This late?"

"It's like a resort over there," he said, wadding up the note. "The horses are treated like pampered guests— lighted stalls, music, the works."

She crossed her arms. "So Will and Annette didn't come back to do what you thought they came back to do."

His expression turned wry. "But that doesn't mean they won't."

"He's a grown man. You can't keep tabs on him all the time."

Greg rubbed his eyes. "I can try."

"Annette is a little immature, but she's a great girl."

"I'd like to believe you."

Lana looked around at the opulence Greg obviously took for granted, and a slow burn of disappointment gnawed at her stomach. He dated women from the classifieds, but he looked down on her friend? What must he think of *her*? She pressed her lips together, biting down painfully. She and Greg were worlds apart—the chances of them becoming involved were nil. In hindsight, her reason for keeping the truth from him about the ad seemed laughable.

"Annette is Coffee Girl," she blurted.

He squinted. "What?"

"Annette is Coffee Girl. I only placed the ad for a roommate. *She* placed the ad that you answered, so I'd appreciate it if you didn't talk about her—"

"Wait a minute." He put his hand to his forehead. "You're telling me that I was supposed to meet Annette that day instead of you?"

She nodded.

"And you didn't place a singles ad?"

"Uh-uh. No offense, but it's not my bag. I didn't tell you because I was afraid you'd try to meet her again, and after what happened at my apartment..."

"You were trying to protect your friend from me?"

"Sort of."

He started laughing, a tired I-don't-believe-this laugh.

Lana straightened. "I don't think it's so funny."

He laughed harder, a long half moan.

"Are you going to let me in on the punch line?"

"Lana, I was answering the singles ad for *Will*."

She blinked. "For Will?"

He gestured wildly. "He brought me an ad he found in a magazine and was fixated on meeting this Coffee Girl. I didn't want him to meet a stranger, so I told him I would check her out first, and if she was nice, I would introduce the two of them."

It was her turn to think. "So you don't answer singles ads?"

He shook his head. "It's, um, not my bag, either."

Lana narrowed her eyes. "Since you never mentioned Will's name to me that day, should I assume you didn't think I was nice?"

His expression changed, the light in his eye shifting from humor to something more primitive. Her pulse quickened. He leaned forward to capture her wrist and gently pulled her toward him.

"That was the problem," he said softly. "Once I saw you, my thoughts turned purely selfish."

She scoffed. "You thought I was a hooker." Then she angled her head. "Of course, I thought you were gay."

His eyebrows dove. *"What?"*

"My ad for a roommate specified females or gay males."

Realization dawned. "So when you asked me if I met all the requirements, you meant...?"

She nodded.

"Does that mean that your roommate is gay?"

She nodded.

He looked dubious. "But I saw you kiss him that day in the shop."

She reached up to trace the outline of his mouth. "Because you spooked me so badly, I had to be sure before I took him back to my apartment."

"And?"

"And," she said, moistening her lips slowly, "I'd rather kiss you."

He lowered his head, his eyes hooded with desire. Their mouths met in a slow, needy kiss that drained her. He moved from her mouth to her jaw, then to her neck, then he slid the spaghetti strap off her shoulder and kissed the pale bare slope. "You are so gorgeous tonight," he murmured against her skin.

"Mmm. Hadn't we better get back to the party?" she whispered, trying to control the waves of shudders his mouth triggered. "I still have some shmoozing to do."

"Relax," he whispered, then slid the other strap from its home. "I already asked my general manager to rerun the project numbers to reflect some of the buildings being preserved."

Lana's heart swelled with relief and happiness. "You did?"

He nodded while he nuzzled her neck. "Mmm-hmm."

"Thank you!" She showered his face with kisses. "Oh, thank you, Greg."

He pulled her face to his, so they were forehead to forehead. "You're welcome. Let's go upstairs."

Her heart thudded in her chest, and she felt herself wavering. God help her, she wanted to experience this man. "What's upstairs?" she asked with a little smile, stalling.

A wicked grin crinkled the corners of his eyes. "My telescope."

She liked him like this. Teasing. Sexy. Science Club guy. Was it possible that here was the real Greg Healey, and the blustery corporate image was just that—an image? A girl could hope. But trust? Lana swallowed hard and studied his chocolate-brown eyes at close range. Could she trust Greg Healey not to break her heart?

Take a chance, her heart whispered. *Maybe he's worth it.*

Reluctant to speak because she wasn't sure what would come out of her mouth, she simply smiled.

WHEN GREG CLOSED his bedroom door and watched Lana pivot slowly, taking in the masculine furnishings, her gaze lingering on the king-size bed, he realized with a start that she was the only woman he'd ever invited to his bedroom. When he'd moved back home seven years ago, he'd been supremely conscious of sharing living space with Will and Yvonne. Frankly, none of the few passable dates he'd been on had warranted an awkward breakfast table scene. Sex had taken place at the home of his dates, and once or twice at a nice hotel. So why now, and why Lana?

As he scrutinized the length of her shapely figure wrapped in the simple black gown, longing stabbed deep in his loins. He'd invited her because she was irresistibly gorgeous, and his desire for her was blurring the edges of his judgment. He had the pressing feeling that if he could only get her out of his system, he could get back to business, back to his life.

She dropped her evening bag and her wrap on the foot of his bed, then walked away from him, climbing two steps to the raised landing. A wall of windows surrounded his telescope where it sat on a tripod. "Nice setup," she murmured, then leaned over to peer into the lens. The unobstructed view of her derriere sent the blood pulsing through his body.

Greg set his jaw, then reached to the wall and extinguished the room's light with the flip of a switch. In the moon-glow streaming through the window, she straightened slightly. "You can see the constellations better in the dark," he explained.

"Oh." Her voice was barely above a whisper.

Greg walked up behind her, his heart thrashing in his ears. He cursed himself for feeling like a jumpy teenager. They were adults, and she knew he'd invited her upstairs to do more than gaze at the stars.

"You have a lovely view of downtown," she said, gesturing to the lights that were even more numerous in celebration of the holidays.

"Sometimes I take the telescope up on the roof," he said. "But the sky is so clear this time of year, I can usually get a good view from here." He swung open the window in front of the telescope, ushering in creaky night sounds and a rush of brisk air. She shivered, and he shrugged out of his jacket, then settled it across her slender shoulders. The fruity scent of her shampoo filled his lungs, and he was struck by an unfamiliar urge to protect her from more than the cold. A ludicrous thought, because Lana Martina could certainly take care of herself. Hadn't he learned that the first day they met?

"What should I be looking for?" she asked, her blond head bent to the lens. "Oh, wow, I can see...*wait a minute.*"

When Greg realized where the telescope was directed, the bottom seemed to fall out of his stomach. His mouth opened and closed, but no sound emerged.

"You've been looking at my apartment building?" Her voice was incredulous and suspicious as she stared at him in the dark.

He swallowed hard. "I've been reviewing your notes and looking over the Hyde Parkland area for traffic patterns. You make it sound as if I've been spying."

Her silence wasn't a comforting reply.

He sighed, exasperated. "You can see for yourself that the scope isn't powerful enough to look into windows or anything."

"I can see my balcony," she said, her voice partly accusing, partly amused.

"I don't even know which balcony is yours." Technically true—he wasn't certain which one was hers, and when he'd realized he could see her building fairly clearly, guilt had kept him from trying to figure it out.

"It's the one with the big wreath on the sliding glass door."

He'd figured as much. "I *wasn't* spying."

"Well, you'd be wasting your time, since I rarely go out on the balcony," she chirped, then bent back to the lens. "So, what can *I* look for? In the sky, that is."

He ignored her barb and tore his gaze from her to take in the dark wintry sky, so black it was nearly purple. He searched for a simple sky mark. "There's the Milky Way galaxy," he said, pointing to the west.

She swung the telescope and looked again. "I see it! It's like a blanket of glitter."

Not an analogy he would have used, but he couldn't help

smiling at her childlike enthusiasm. "At the mouth of the Milky Way is the constellation Aquila, then it becomes most dense at Cygnus, then begins to peter out at the Charioteer."

Lana swung the scope slowly, following the galaxy that was millions of miles long. And he studied her, the lines of her lithe arms, the slope of her shoulder, the curve of her hip. Her hair and skin glowed luminous in the low light. Mere inches separated their bodies, and the distance shrank as he succumbed to the pull emanating from her—

"Greg?"

He started. "What?"

"I asked if you wanted to be an astronaut when you were little."

A tiny laugh escaped him. "For about a month. The summer I was ten my career aspirations ran the gamut from professional baseball pitcher to race car driver."

"When did you become interested in astronomy?"

"It was my mother's passion," he admitted.

She straightened and turned to look at him. "Your mother must have been a fascinating woman."

He nodded, the memories still bittersweet. "She was. We all miss her, especially Will."

"I can imagine," she murmured, her voice wistful. "I miss my mother, and she lives only a day's drive away."

"Do you see her often?"

"Well, Janet sells real estate, so it's hard for her to take time off, and now I have the shop..."

Her voice trailed off, and he had the strangest feeling she was making excuses for her mother, not for herself.

"Anyway, I can't wait until Christmas Eve. We're going to make a gingerbread house and—I'm sorry, I'm rambling."

His ego swelled a tiny bit at the idea that her nervousness stemmed from being in his bedroom.

"Greg," she said, turning toward him. "I don't think coming up here was such a good idea."

He hadn't realized how much he wanted her in his bed until faced with the prospect of her walking out. A murmur of protest emerged from his tight throat. "Why don't we double-check?" he asked, then pulled her against him for a long, breathless kiss.

Two seconds into the kiss, it was clear that despite her misgivings about the wisdom of their actions, she was where she wanted to be. Their mouths and bodies melded perfectly. Greg planted his feet on either side of her, creating an intimate cradle for her to lean into. Adrenaline and desire pumped through his body at the knowledge that they would soon be intimately entwined.

He broke their kiss long enough to lean over and scoop her into his arms. Romantic gesture aside, carrying her to the bed simply seemed...expeditious. He carried her down the two steps, then crossed to the massive bed in two strides. His control already precarious, stretching out next to her on the cool comforter sent a wave of longing barbing through his body. Her soft moan of acquiescence had him setting his jaw in restraint.

His eyes had adjusted to the dark. Moonlight streamed in through the open window, casting a sheen upon the floor and the bed. She lay slightly diagonally, her chin tipped up expectantly, her chest rising and falling rapidly. So lovely. So beguiling. Greg feasted upon the sight of her, overcome by the enormous swell of passion that surged through him. "Have I told you that you're the most desirable woman I've ever met?" he murmured, then lowered a kiss to her jawline.

"Yes, but I bet you say that to all the women." Her voice

was the sexy rasp of a woman who knew she had a man by the hormones.

He moaned denial, relieved that she hadn't bolted from his room. Anticipation coursed through him. He held an exquisite gift, which he intended to unwrap with infinite care. He eased his suit jacket from her shoulders, lowering one strap, then the other to make way for his tongue. Gathering her into his arms, he lowered his mouth to nuzzle just above the low neckline of her gown, gratified when she arched into him, and that her movement tugged the dress down so far that the hard peaks of her breasts popped into view. Greg accepted her subtle invitation with fervor, laving the pearled tips while a delicate citrus scent lurking in the valley between her breasts teased his senses higher.

His control was slipping badly. He buried his face against her skin, marveling how he could feel so safe and so anxious at the same time. As alarms sounded in his brain, another sensation registered. A distant noise—a voice. He stiffened at the sound of his name being called from the first floor.

"Gregory?"

Greg hesitated, then lifted his head. "It's Will." Remorse knifed through him. How could he make sure his brother wasn't...doing *this* if he was in his bedroom with Lana...doing *this*? He heaved a sigh and sat up, ignoring the ache in his loins. "I'm sorry. I can't do this while Will is around. I feel like I need to set an example."

She pushed into a sitting position with her back to him, adjusting the bodice of her dress. "I understand."

Her voice was strained and shaky. Was she upset at being interrupted, or relieved?

"Gregory?"

Frustration clawed at him as he stood and shrugged into his jacket. "Let's go back to your place," he suggested, reaching out but stopping short of touching her shoulder, "or get a room."

"No," she said quietly, then stood abruptly, smoothing her hand over the skirt of her gown as she retrieved her purse. "I'd better be leaving."

"Gregory? Are you here?"

Greg pulled his hand down over his face. He wanted to throw caution and responsibilities to the wind, then throw Lana on the bed and ravish her. Instead, he inhaled deeply and did what he always did—the right thing. "I'll take you home," he conceded. He'd probably be thanking Will tomorrow for the timely interruption, but he still had tonight to get through.

Her wrap had fallen to the floor at the corner of the bed. Greg bent to pick up the silky length of fabric, and extended it to her in the semidarkness. She reached for it, her eyes averted, but he held on, engaging in a slight tug-of-war until she looked up. "I'm sorry. My life isn't always my own. I have responsibilities." Even as the words left his mouth, he recognized their meaning in a larger context. *If things were different...*

But things weren't different. Lana's eyes were luminous in the low lighting. Her pale hair glowed, the ends curling around her slender neck. "You don't owe me anything, Greg."

At her detached tone, he released the wrap. She draped it over her arm carefully, then walked to the door, just as if nothing had transpired between them.

He clenched his jaw to the point of pain. Then again, in her opinion, maybe nothing had.

20

LANA WAS IN THE THROES of a full-body yawn when the telltale sound of Annette's double ring at the back door reverberated through the empty shop. Thanks to last night's encounter with Greg, Lana had become acquainted with every square inch of her lumpy mattress after she'd gotten home and crawled into bed.

She walked toward the back door, steeling for Annette's certain barrage. When they had emerged from Greg's room last night, Annette's eyes had been full of questions. Will had been more direct.

"What were you all doing, Gregory?"

"Looking at the stars, pal."

"Gregory has a big telescope," Will had informed Annette, whose eyebrows seemed to have frozen high on her forehead as she studied Lana. Thank goodness Will had then announced that Annette was Coffee Girl, and the four had laughed over the mix-up.

Annette didn't get the chance to drill Lana afterward because Greg drove and Will rode along to take them both home. Lana's apartment was closer, and after a tense ride during which she and Greg exchanged only a dozen words, she'd practically vaulted from the car.

Now, forcing a cheerful smile, she undid the latch. "Good morning."

"Yes, it is," Annette sang, blowing in on an early morning chill, carrying warm delicacies covered with fogged-up wax paper.

Lana ignored the obvious invitation to discussion. "Smells de-lish."

"I was inspired." More singing.

She sighed and took the tray, conceding defeat. "Let's see...you're in love?"

"How can you tell?"

"Wild guess."

Annette grinned. "Isn't Will the kindest, handsomest man you've ever seen?"

"Yes." At least the "handsome" part ran in the family.

"He's all I think about, Lana. It's like we were meant to be. Imagine, if you and Greg weren't working together on this rezoning thing, Will and I would never have met."

"You would have met sooner if Greg hadn't interfered," Lana pointed out.

The redhead shrugged. "Things happen for a reason."

Did they? Lana wondered. She had always thought so, but what good could possibly come of meeting Greg Healey? Even if he decided to spare her business, what about her heart?

"You like him, don't you?"

Lana snapped back to the present. "Will? I think he's a great guy."

"No, I mean Greg."

"Oh. Greg and I are...opposites," she said lamely.

"I think he likes you, too."

"But I don't—"

"Lana, did Will and I interrupt something last night?"

"Don't you have more trays to carry in? I suspect today will be hopping with all the last-minute shoppers."

Annette angled her head, but finally nodded. "You're

right—I'll get the rest. Oh, are you definitely going to be closed tomorrow?"

She nodded. "I'm going to deliver the gifts for the children in the morning, then do some last-minute decorating, and make a big Christmas Eve dinner before my mother arrives."

"Will invited me to have dinner with him and Greg and Yvonne."

If she hadn't had her own plans, Lana might have been envious. But the Healey brothers couldn't be more different. Will was looking for someone to include in his life. Greg was looking for someone to include in his bed... But only when no one else was in the house, she thought wryly.

"That's nice," she said. "But are you sure you aren't moving too fast, Annette?"

Astonishment widened her friend's features. "Lana, life is short. When love finds you, you shouldn't waste time. I'll be back with the cranberry truffles."

Such a simple concept, Lana thought as she watched her friend walk away, her every step punctuated with a happy bounce. When love finds you, you shouldn't waste time. But did love find everyone? And what if your every waking thought was occupied by a person who you knew didn't feel the same? And what if that person held your future in their hands?

Holy heartbreak.

"ALL NEXT WEEK OFF, sir—I mean, Mr. Healey? For everyone in the company?"

Greg nodded his approval at Peg's more casual address. "Yes. Do you think you can contact everyone at home?" It was, after all, Saturday morning. He and Peg were the only two in the office. He'd showered, but hadn't bothered to shave since the party last night. Hadn't bothered to sleep, either.

"Sure, Mr. Healey. I'll use the calling tree we have in place in case we close due to bad weather."

"Then I'll leave the matter in your capable hands. Merry Christmas."

She blinked, then smiled. "Merry Christmas, Mr. Healey."

At a rap on the door, they both looked up. Art Payton stood in the doorway.

"Got a minute?"

"Sure," Greg said, waving him in. Peg slipped out and closed the door behind her.

Art dropped his considerable bulk into a chair. "I got a call this morning from Mitch Ryder, the largest developer who's shown interest in the Hyde Parkland project."

Dread curled in his stomach, but Greg nodded. "Go on."

"Well, seems as though a couple of big apartment buildings are available in Frankfort. Ryder thinks he can convert them to condos. Trouble is, he can't handle both jobs at once, so it's either the Hyde parcel or the Frankfort parcel."

"And he needs to know right away," Greg said.

"As soon as possible. He'd rather do business here."

"And if we make changes to the plans at this point?"

"We'll lose Ryder."

"But we can find another developer."

"In time. But why risk it? You can have a home run when this rezoning goes through by sticking to your original plan. Or you can give in to the merchants, and settle for a lot less money coming in over a longer period of time."

"Either way we won't go bankrupt."

"But with Ryder, you can retire. Buy a sailboat. Cruise the South Seas."

Greg respected Art's candor—the man worked on salary,

so he was speaking from an unbiased viewpoint. "The rezoning vote will take place the second week of January."

"I can hold Ryder off until then," Art promised, "but no longer." He pushed himself to his feet and headed for the door. "Greg?"

Greg looked up.

"This is no time to start being Mr. Nice Guy." Art lifted his hand in a wave, then swaggered out the door.

Greg tossed down his pen, then scooted his chair back with a frustrated sigh. Hell, if he could convince Lana to go along with the rezoning, they'd have enough money to do whatever they wanted. She'd never miss the coffee shop. He frowned. *They?*

A dry laugh escaped him. He knew Lana Martina well enough to know that the way to her heart was not through money derived at the expense of things she held dear. His frown deepened. *The way to her heart.* Where had that come from? Besides, Lana had told him she wasn't interested in a relationship. How could he possibly walk away from the chance of a lifetime in return for—what? A few weeks of torrid lovemaking? And who's to say she even wanted to have an affair?

The phone rang, and he answered since Peg was probably busy spreading Christmas cheer to the employees. "Greg Healey."

"Greg, it's Charlie Andrews."

Greg grinned when he heard the voice of a buddy from law school he'd run into last week while playing hooky at the courthouse. "Hey, Charlie."

"Only you would be working on the Saturday before Christmas."

Greg laughed. "What about you?"

"And me. Listen, I've been thinking about our conversation last week, and you hinting at making a move into the courtroom."

His pulse picked up. "And?"

"And I have a proposition for you. The DA's office is recovering from some political infighting. To make a long story short, they're looking for a few good men."

Greg sat forward in his chair, barely able to contain his excitement. "But Charlie, I have no courtroom experience."

"I know, but the money is barely enough to live on, so it evens out. In fact, I'm sure you'll be up to speed long before your salary is. The office has some big cases coming up in the next six months. Could be career makers for a guy with the right stuff who's willing to work on the cheap."

"I don't know what to say, Charlie." Every muscle in his body screamed yes.

"Say you'll think about it over the holidays. I'll catch up with you after the New Year."

"Great. And thanks."

"Merry Christmas, man."

"To you, too."

Greg returned the receiver slowly, pleasure pooling in his stomach. A chance to work in the DA's office, doing what he'd always wanted to do.

But for pauper's pay. He sighed, then pushed himself to his feet and walked over to the garland-decorated window to stare at the courthouse roof. If the rezoning proposal went through, he'd be a rich man. A rich man who could prosecute landmark cases without worrying about providing for himself and for Will—and, now with a girlfriend in the picture, perhaps Will's offspring. His brother couldn't raise a family on the minimum wage he earned.

And then there was Lana. And her violet eyes. And her bleeding heart.

He groaned as Art's parting words came back to him. After all these years, what a bad time to have grown a conscience.

21

LANA WOKE ON Christmas Eve morning with little-girl anticipation at seeing her mother again. She smiled wide as she stretched, then jumped into the shower, humming Christmas tunes under her breath. Janet already would have left for the eight-hour trip north. She'd told Lana the last time they'd spoken on the phone to expect her around four in the afternoon, which gave Lana plenty of time to deliver the gifts to the children's center where a breakfast for the kids was being held.

She still marveled at Greg's generosity. Alex had teased her that he was simply trying to butter her up, but she liked to think that his heart had truly gone out to the children.

She had to make two trips with a huge bag of gifts strapped to her moped, but it was more than worth it to see the looks on the faces of the children. Her own problems— real and perceived—seemed petty next to the trials that other people experienced day in and day out.

Even though the Christmas card she'd mailed to her father a month ago had been returned yesterday with no forwarding address, at least she still had Janet. Even if her business were shut down in the next few months, she'd still find a way to make a living and eventually repay her debt. Even if Greg Healey didn't care for her, she had her health and good friends around her. Everything was relative.

So with much effort, she quashed the emotions that seemed to have careened out of control since the episode in his room two nights ago. Her left brain told her there was no future with Greg Healey. But her right brain had wrapped its synapses around the words Annette had spoken yesterday. *When love finds you, you shouldn't waste time.*

She hadn't shared her burgeoning feelings for Greg with anyone, although Annette suspected something was going on. Alex had asked a few vague questions about the rezoning proposal the last time they'd talked on the phone, but was preoccupied with overseeing the Christmas rush at Tremont's and with moving into her new home. Rich had left Friday and wouldn't return until the thirtieth. Harry was no help whatsoever.

But she planned to tell Janet about Greg, another reason she was looking forward to their time together. Her mother would want all the details, would want to sit up until two in the morning in their pj's, talking about life and love and men. And maybe in the course of trying to express her thoughts about Greg, some unforgivable wart on his character would be revealed, some defect that would neutralize these...stirrings of her heart. Janet would tease her mercilessly because Lana had never before been in...deep like this. She'd scattered candles around the kitchen and living room. Her mother loved candles, and Elvis's "Blue Christmas" album, which Lana had found on CD, along with Jim Reeves and Lou Rawls, two more of her mother's faves. She loaded the CDs into the stereo, smiling as the strains of the old recordings came over her speakers. She'd be tired of them by the time Janet arrived, but it put her in the mood to finish decorating.

Harry wore a tolerant smile as she dressed him in a Santa suit. "Behave while Mom's here, okay?" She stuffed his hard plastic doll manhood into the red pants and pulled the hem of the coat down for more camouflage. By two o'clock she had hung garlands from every surface, set luminaries in her windows, removed the turkey from the oven, and had begun baking the walls for the gingerbread house they would build together. Just looking over the ingredients sent a little tremor of happiness through her chest—gumdrops and sugar cubes and squeeze tubes of colored icing. Nothing said Christmas like the gingerbread houses she and her mother used to make when Lana was little.

While the gingerbread baked, she showered and changed into a black velvet jumpsuit, then dabbed perfume behind her ears. Janet had sent her a rhinestone candy-cane pin for Christmas last year from the Bahamas, and it showed up well against the dark fabric. The gingerbread came out more perfectly than she'd ever seen it. A good omen, she thought, smiling to herself while keeping one eye on the clock. One more hour. She let the slabs cool on the breakfast bar while she put together the rest of their feast.

The phone rang, and she picked it up while sliding the asparagus into the oven. "Hello?"

"Hey, it's Alex. Merry Christmas."

"Merry Christmas to you, too."

"I just called to check in. I hear Elvis in the background, so your mom must be there."

She glanced at the clock—3:45. "Not yet, but she should be here any minute."

"Okay." Her friend was trying hard to sound casual, bless her. "Jack and I are spending the night at Dad's, if you need anything."

"I won't, but thanks."

"Sure. And don't forget about our New Year's Eve party next Sunday."

"Are you sure you want to have a party in your new house after you've just moved in?"

"It'll be fun. And it's shaping up to be a good-size crowd. Jack's brother will be there, and his wife. You'll like them."

"If it's all couples, maybe I should pass."

"Don't be silly. Derek's wife has a friend in from Atlanta, and some of the people I work with are coming. Don't forget to invite your roommate. Oh, and Annette and her new beau, of course."

Lana waited as two seconds passed, then three, four, five.

"And you can invite a date if you like."

She smiled into the phone. "Really? Whoever would I ask?"

"Anyone," Alex said in her most innocent voice. "Hey, since Greg Healey's brother is coming with Annette, why don't you ask him? I know Jack would like to see him again."

A smirk pulled back one side of Lana's mouth. "Hmm. I'll probably just ride with Rich, if he can come. But thanks for offering."

"Okay. Well, have a good time with your mother," Alex said.

"I will," Lana said. "I'll call you later in the week."

She hung up and snacked on a celery stick dipped in peanut butter while she put the finishing touches on the decorations. She lit all the candles and lowered the lights to show off the masterpiece of a Christmas tree that was leaning ever so slightly. And she rearranged her mother's gifts so that the bows were perky. At the last minute she remembered the two disposable cameras she'd bought and put them on the counter so she could take pictures as soon as Janet arrived.

And she tried not to check the clock too often. Four-ten. Four-seventeen. Four-twenty-four. At four-thirty she considered blowing out some of the wilting candles, and turned off all the warming burners for the food.

At five-fifteen the phone rang again. Lana snapped it up. "Hello?"

The crackly noise of a cellular phone with bad reception sounded over the line. "Lana, darling, it's Mother."

Her heart raced. Janet only called herself "Mother" under dire circumstances. "Mom? Is something wrong?" Her father's Christmas card had been returned. Was he okay?

"No, nothing's wrong. You're such a worrywart."

A by-product of growing up fast. "Are you held up in traffic?"

"Darling, I'm afraid I'm not going to be able to make it this year."

Lana swallowed hard and blinked back sudden hot tears. "Oh?" was all she could manage to say.

"Yes, dear. At the last minute, Larry got this fabulous deal on a cruise to Cancún, and we're getting ready to set sail."

"Set sail?" She cleared her throat of the emotion that lodged there. "I wish you had called. I...wish you had called."

"I'm sorry, darling. We had to leave in a rush, and this is the first chance I've had to ring you. I hope you didn't go to any trouble."

Lana looked around the sparkly, glittery apartment, awash with holiday magic, with Elvis crooning in the background, and savory scents coming from the kitchen. "No. No trouble."

"Oh, there's our boarding call, dear. I have to go. I'll send you a nice blanket or something from Mexico."

Or something.

"Lana, are you there?"

"I'm here," she croaked. "Have a good time."

"We will—"

The line went dead. Lana stared at the phone until a

piercing tone sounded and a voice informed her that if she would like to make a call, please hang up and try again. She dropped the phone on the love seat, then slowly walked around the room. The cooling gingerbread house walls had developed half-inch wide cracks. How fitting.

She tore off the chimney and chewed on it as she wandered around, blowing out candles. She attributed the haze and the smoky odor to the extinguished candles, until she realized the asparagus was burning. When she opened the oven, the green spears were black—and on fire. Lana shrieked, then yanked a mitt from the counter, pulled out the flaming dish and carried it to the sliding glass door. The balcony was antique wrought iron—fireproof. She set the casserole dish on the floor and jerked her hand away, sucking on a burned thumb.

Then the tears came. She hugged the oven mitt to her aching chest and wept as she looked out over a glittery Lexington, where normal people were tucked in their warm houses having dinner and exchanging gifts with loved ones. How big a loser was she if even her parents didn't want to be with her on Christmas Eve?

In the light of day, she could nonchalantly announce she was happy living alone. But at this forlorn moment, she felt as if she were being paid a courtesy visit from the Ghost of Christmas Future: a vision of her at eighty-five, living alone save for Harry and seventeen cats.

She'd trained herself to believe, especially over the past few years, that she could only truly rely on herself. But her tears were tangible proof that she needed someone else to share her life, to fill the void in her heart that in rare moments of despair seemed bottomless.

She wasn't sure how long she stood there in the cold. It could have been ten minutes or an hour. The next stimulus she was aware of was a buzzing noise inside her apartment.

Afraid she might have set something else on fire and triggered an alarm, Lana rushed back inside to the tune of her doorbell ringing. Puzzled, she pressed a watery eye to the peephole.

Greg stood in the hallway. Her breath froze in her chest. What was he doing here?

He knocked on the door sharply. "Lana? It's Greg. Are you okay? Lana?"

She swung open the door.

Greg had his hand raised, poised to knock again. He looked out of place in the musty hallway, tall and broad and sexy, wearing dark slacks and a white shirt and a black leather jacket, smelling like a man and sporting a tentative smile. He was the most welcome sight imaginable.

"Wh-what are you doing here?"

His brown eyes narrowed. "You've been crying."

She swiped at her eyes. "I, uh, burned something in the oven and the smoke got in my eyes. What are you doing here?"

He shrugged, and shifted foot to foot. "Did your mother arrive?"

"Um, no, she had a change in plans—" Lana stopped, then looked to the sliding glass door and back to Greg. "You saw me on the balcony, didn't you."

"By accident."

"Your eye fell against your telescope that just happened to be trained on my balcony?"

A flush climbed his face. "You were standing outside in the cold for over an hour. I called, but your phone is off the hook."

She glanced to her couch where the phone lay, emitting a fast busy signal.

"Is anything wrong?" he asked.

A hysterical little laugh bubbled out. At the moment

there was more wrong in her life than was right, and this man was responsible for at least half of it. Suddenly bombarded with the concern in his eyes, the disappointment of her mother's call, and the melancholy strains of Jim Reeves crooning "Silver Bells" in the background, Lana burst into tears.

22

GREG STOOD STOCK-STILL, watching the sudden display of waterworks, at a complete loss. How did women *do* that? He fumbled in his back pocket for a handkerchief and offered it to her. She was really boo-hooing now, and at least two neighbors stuck their heads into the hall to stare at him. "May I come in?" he asked.

She nodded and stepped aside, her shoulders heaving with the great mouthfuls of air she gulped.

Greg walked in and carefully closed the door, his pupils dilating in response to the wonderland of decorations. The air was hazy, probably from all the half-burned candles sitting around the room. His nostrils flared at the aroma of food—burned and otherwise—emanating from the kitchen. From the surroundings and Lana's dressy outfit and her tears, it was clear that she had been stood up. Stood up by her mother on Christmas Eve. His heart squeezed for her, and he resisted the urge to fold her into his arms.

Just a little while ago he'd been pacing in his room, agonizing over how to tell Lana that his response to the council would be uncompromising—pass the rezoning proposal as is, or he would be forced to hike the shop owners' rents to offset his company's losses. Higher rents would force some merchants out of business—a no-win situation. The city council would pass the rezoning plan, but he'd be painted as the bad guy. Still, it would be worth the intense unpop-

ularity if the deal put him one step closer to that job Charlie
had promised him.

Lana, of course, would hate him.

He'd been drawn to the window, to the telescope. Ab-
surdly, looking at her apartment building made him feel
closer to her. He'd even practiced telling her, trying to put
a good spin on his words: *You're an accountant, Lana. You
know this is a simple case of sacrificing the needs of a few to sat-
isfy the needs of many.*

Yes, she would say. *You're right, Greg. Now make love to me.*

He'd laughed at his own foolishness. And when she'd
emerged from the sliding glass door, he'd nearly knocked
over the telescope. Then she'd remained on the balcony, in
the cold and without that ridiculous dalmation coat, and
he'd known something was wrong.

But he hadn't counted on an emotional dilemma. Now,
powerless to stem her tears, Greg bit down on the inside of
his cheek and waited for her to take a breath. "If you don't
have other plans, come back to the house with me for
Christmas Eve dinner."

She stopped crying and hiccuped, then blew her nose
heartily into his handkerchief. She was considering his
question—knowing her, spinning through the ramifica-
tions, looking for an ulterior motive.

"Annette is already there," he cajoled. "And you can
meet Yvonne and her brother."

She dabbed at her eyes and sniffed mightily.

"And besides," he added. "I'd like it very much if you'd
come."

At the widening of her tear-streaked eyes, he thought
he'd gone too far, almost admitted something he didn't
even want to admit to himself—that he had grown attached
to her violet eyes and her quick wit and her funky clothes.

"Otherwise, I'm going to feel like a fifth wheel at the table," he continued with a little laugh.

"Oh," she croaked, then blew her nose again. "Well, it's nice of you to include me, but—" she gestured vaguely toward the kitchen "—I have so much food here, and I don't think I'd be very good company."

"No one should be alone on Christmas Eve."

She laughed, a strained, high-pitched sound. "I don't suppose you'd consider staying and having dinner with me? Overcooked turkey and asparagus flambé?"

He blinked. Dining together *alone* on Christmas Eve smacked of...intimacy. "Well, I'm expected back at home. Will and Annette—"

"I forgot," she cut in with a little wave. "You're chaperoning."

He smirked at her teasing tone, but was glad beyond comprehension that her mood had lightened. "I'm not chaperoning. I'm just...keeping an eye on them."

She leaned toward him, her eyes dancing with mischief. "Do you know how much sex they could be having right now?"

His body leapt to rapt attention at her words and her proximity. Every muscle strained toward her, pulled by some invisible force that baffled him. "How much?" he murmured, no longer able to resist touching her.

He opened his arms, and she came into them with a little groan. Greg wrapped his arms around her, closed his eyes and inhaled the scent of her—fruit and...smoke? The burned food, of course. He smiled into her hair while his chest swelled with a firestorm of emotion, including sympathy for her. How could a mother not appreciate having this beautiful, intelligent creature for a daughter? Overcome with the urge to protect her, he kissed her hard and kneaded her back. The fuzzy nap of her jumpsuit felt luxurious under his fingers, smooth and sexy and inviting. His sex hardened and ached for release.

Days of pent-up desire and near misses hurried their movements. He didn't know how they made it to her bedroom, but he knew he would forever remember the way they'd tumbled onto her bed, tugging at clothes, wordless in their need and urgency to have each other. Within seconds, they were stripped to their underwear—Lana hadn't been wearing a bra.

He pulled away long enough to take in the sight of her, lying on her side, the curve of her hip rising above the dip of her waist, the fullness of her breasts rising and falling in her breathlessness. Black bikini panties were a perfect contrast to the pale, flat plane of her stomach. Her legs extended long and lean and limber. Greg's erection, already straining painfully, surged anew, prompting him to shed his boxers. Speechless with need, he turned his mind and body over to automatic, kissing and massaging her exposed skin. He acknowledged on a subconscious level that one of the emotions driving him to please her was regret—regret that he would be the next person who would disappoint her. He poured all his energy into lavishing on her body the attention she deserved. An advance apology, of sorts. With a groan, he slipped his hand inside the scrap of black fabric between her legs.

Already near the point of sensory overload, Lana cried out in response to his gentle probing and opened her legs to accommodate one, then two long fingers. Moving with his slow rhythm, she felt an intense orgasm flowering, blooming deep in her womb. Part of her wanted him to prolong the deft exploration, but part of her wanted him to take her quickly to end the sensual torture. Then without warning, her muscles contracted around his muscular fingers, unleashing a tide of pleasure so fierce, she dug her fingernails into his shoulders. "Greg...Greg...oh, Greg." Bright spots of light swirled behind her eyes, and her body convulsed as the orgasm claimed her, wave by wave.

When the world righted itself, she was primed for his remarkable body to join hers. He was the personification of Adam—tall, broad, lean and equipped. Every movement displaced toned muscle. Lana watched, fascinated, engrossed, thrilled.

While he rolled a condom onto his raging erection, she lifted her hips and shimmied out of the panties, her inhibitions long gone. She reached for him, pulling at his shoulders, levering her hips beneath his.

His back was moist with perspiration, as was his brow. His breath escaped in staccato bursts as he gathered her beneath him, vying for the best angle. His erection, hard and thick with want, prodded her folds. She waited for his sensual invasion, her breath caught in her thudding chest. Then he entered her with one deliberate thrust.

She sucked in a sharp breath at the incredible fullness his body added to hers. Strange, but in those few seconds of intense physical union, Lana was struck by her participation in this ritual that had made the world go around since the dawn of mankind. Never had she felt such a connection with nature and with her base emotions. She kneaded his back, adopting his slow, thorough rhythm, meeting his hip thrusts with her own.

"Amazing," he whispered, his breathing compromised. "So...good."

Age-old female satisfaction curled in her chest. "Love me, Greg...*harder.*"

He slid his hands under her hips, cradling her bottom with his large hands, and obliged, plunging in and out like a piston, faster and harder, until his body went rigid and a sharp guttural moan tore from his mouth. Triumph flooded her limbs as the ragged sighs of his release filled her ears. At last he quieted, sagging against her, raining exhausted kisses on her throat before he rolled away to lie beside her on the rumpled comforter.

Amazing, she seconded silently, sinking deeper into the softness at her back. Her body hummed with fulfillment and discovery, and other sensations too complicated to delve into. Their lovemaking was a result of unrealized chemistry and loneliness—no need to overanalyze the obvious. *Keep it casual*, she told herself. He was probably already regretting what had happened.

"Are you hungry?" she whispered to the ceiling, then braced for his excuse to leave as soon as possible.

"Starved."

She rolled over on her side to study his profile—strong brow, jutting nose, square jaw. How easy it would be to fall for this man.

"Greg, do you have plans for New Year's Eve?" she asked.

He turned his head, and for a few seconds she was afraid she'd pushed too far, assumed too much.

"Lana," he said, his voice raspy. "I..."

Her heart withdrew, preparing for rejection. He wasn't looking for a relationship, he would remind her. He had more important obligations—his business, his brother. He stared at her, and she tried to banish the thought that he was the most handsome man she'd ever known. And their chemistry—holy high voltage! She could barely keep from touching him. But common sense told her that their raging passion would soon burn itself out.

Now that the conquest was over, had his interest in her already been extinguished?

"What?" she asked, then closed her eyes. The sooner he put his feelings—or lack thereof—on the table, the sooner she could dispel the fairy tales that had infiltrated her holiday-weakened mind.

"I, um..." He cleared his throat. "No, as a matter of fact, I don't have plans for New Year's Eve."

Her heart lurched crazily. "How about Christmas morning?" she murmured, braver now. She slid her hand over his rock-hard stomach.

The flash of his white teeth coincided with his surrendering groan. "This is going to be hard to explain to Will."

She laughed, a little afraid of how much his words buoyed her. "You'll think of something."

23

EVEN IN THE CROWDED great room of the Stillmans' new home, Greg knew the precise moment that Lana arrived at the New Year's Eve party. The energy in the air increased markedly, ratcheting up the temperature. Her voice reached him before he saw her—a lyrical, uplifting sound that elicited involuntary responses from his nether regions.

They'd decided after spending Christmas Eve together that it would be prudent to put their relationship on hold until after the conflict of interest passed. No good would come of the shop owners finding out she was sleeping with the enemy. But Lana had asked Greg to attend the New Year's Eve party, anyway, promising to flirt with him from across the room.

The week since he'd left her bed had seemed like an eternity. The past few days he'd been plagued by the potentially life-changing decisions he had to make that would have been straightforward just a few weeks ago. If he remained firm on the rezoning plan, he'd pocket a small fortune. The money would allow him to accept a low-paying entry-level position in the DA's office. And a neglected area of downtown Lexington would receive an economic boost.

So why couldn't he find the nerve to tell Lana? And why did the faces of the Hyde Parkland shop owners haunt him—the dubious smirk on Marshall Ballou's face, the wrinkled concern on Vic the Barber's ugly mug, the nervous twitch on Maxie Dodd's flour-covered features.

Lana came into view, stealing his breath. He couldn't fail to notice the trusting optimism on her sweet face.

What should be a slam-dunk decision was being blocked by a pair of violet-colored eyes. She smiled at him from across the room, a private I-know-what-you-look-like-naked smile that made breathing more difficult. Greg swallowed hard and tried to ignore the stab of disappointment when she turned to greet someone else.

"Greg Healey?" a man's voice asked behind him.

Greg turned to see his host, Alex's husband, striding up. "Jack Stillman."

Dressed in jeans and an untucked shirt, the big man looked more like the UK football icon he'd been in college than a partner in a successful advertising firm. Greg extended his hand. "I remember you from the university."

"I remember you, too," Jack said with a lifted eyebrow. "We've both changed a little, eh?"

Greg nodded, wondering if Jack, like everyone else, had thought he was a jerk in college, and if the man knew about his disastrous first meeting with Lana.

"Lana explained the mix-up about the classified ads," Jack said, as if he'd read Greg's mind.

Heat suffused his face. "Damn embarrassing."

Jack laughed heartily. "Reminds me of when I met Alex. I thought she was an IRS agent coming to audit the advertising agency, so I laid it on pretty thick about how we were barely able to pay the light bill, etcetera. Then I found out that she was from Tremont's and she'd come by early to scout me and the agency before I pitched the account."

Greg grinned and pulled on his chin. "Ouch."

"Yeah. And she's been a thorn in my side ever since," he said good-naturedly, then indicated his striking wife with a nod. "But it's worth every minute of the pain."

Greg's gaze involuntarily strayed to Lana. She was stunning in snug pink jeans and an oversize white shirt cinched with a silver belt.

"Lana's a great gal, man. Tread lightly, if you know what's good for you."

He frowned. "I'm not going to do anything to hurt Lana."

Jack laughed. "Lana can take care of herself. I was talking about saving yourself." He clapped Greg on the back. "Enjoy the party, man."

Greg didn't have time to ponder Jack's words, because a redhead with harsh makeup slinked up to him, smiling wide. Her lipstick was drawn outside of her mouth, making her look as if she were all gums. "Hello," she said silkily, batting tarantula-like eyelashes.

"Hello," he said with a tight smile, his mind so... elsewhere.

"THIS IS DEREK STILLMAN, Jack's brother," Alex said, making introductions. "And his wife, Janine."

A very *pregnant* Janine, Lana noted with a smile. "It's nice to meet you." They made a fabulous-looking couple—she the blond flower-child, he the brawny businessman. Newlyweds, she remembered Alex saying. Something about Derek standing in for his brother Jack as best man at a wedding and falling in love with the bride.

"And this is my friend Manny Oliver from Atlanta," Janine said, gesturing to a tall blond man, impeccably dressed.

Lana shook hands all around, immediately liking Manny's friendly demeanor. He worked in the hospitality industry, he said. Hotel management. He seemed impressed that she owned her own business—for how long, though, was another story.

"Everyone, this is my friend and roommate, Rich Enderling," she said, repeating the introductions.

Rich and Derek exchanged a few humorous observations about Rich's employer, Phillips Foods, which was also a client of Jack and Derek's advertising agency. Then Rich extended his hand to Manny.

Lana noticed the slightest pause when the men's hands met, and the split second of awareness that ricocheted between them. Was it possible that Manny was gay?

Yes, she realized a few seconds later when the men extricated themselves unobtrusively from the little knot of people and moved in the direction of the chilled buffet on a granite-topped sideboard. Lana angled her head, recalling Rich's wistful words as he stood in front of her kitchen window. *I have a good feeling about Lexington, Lana, like something significant is going to happen for me here.* And perhaps it just had, she acknowledged, as Rich laughed in response to something Manny had said.

"So what do you think about the house?" Alex whispered near her ear.

Lana lifted her hand to indicate...everything. The high ceilings, the elaborate fixtures, the sumptuous natural materials. Her friend had exquisite taste, and the money to indulge her knack. "The house is spectacular, as you well know."

Alex's smile was mischievous. "I was just curious, seeing as you've barely taken your eyes off Greg Healey since you arrived."

Lana blushed, resisting the urge to seek him out. "I didn't even ride with Greg, Alex. Don't make a big deal out of the fact that I invited him."

"So what's really going on with the two of you?" Alex asked, sipping from a mixed drink.

If Lana knew herself, she'd be tempted to tell her best friend. Christmas Eve night had been magical, not to mention exhausting. Greg had left the next morning after daybreak, limping slightly. Lana had drifted through the day in an endorphin-induced haze. He had called twice during the week, both times when she'd been out, but had left brief messages of no consequence. Still, the sound of his voice had sent her pulse racing. And every night after she'd closed the shop, she'd invented a reason to step out onto the balcony for a few minutes, reveling in the remote but delicious possibility that his eyes were on her.

"Lana?"

She jerked back to the present. "What?"

Alex tsk-tsked. "You've fallen for him, haven't you."

After looking around to make sure they were out of earshot of everyone else, she smiled sheepishly. "That depends. What was it like when you fell for Jack?"

A dreamy look came over her friend's face. "Oh, I merely thought about him every waking second, and the sight of him made me forget my name."

Lana winced. "I was afraid you were going to say that."

"I knew it! It's about time you fell in love."

"Shh! Keep your voice down!"

Alex grinned and did a little dance that Lana attributed to the rum in her cola. Then her friend stopped, mid-jig. "But what does this mean for the rezoning proposal?"

Lana studied her coffee-stained fingernails. "We agreed not to see each other until after the vote on the rezoning proposal, to avoid any appearance of impropriety. We're meeting with Ms. Wheeler the day after tomorrow to review all angles of the proposal and to submit our final arguments." Then she sighed. "But to be honest, Alex, I've been thinking for some time that Greg's plan is the best chance the Hyde Parkland area has for resurrection."

Alex's eyes widened. "But your arguments against the development were so convincing."

She shook her head. "My arguments were based on historical factors with a dozen variables that differ from this situation. My projections could be wrong. I think I was more fired up by the way the proposal was being railroaded through than by the proposal itself."

"Are you sure Greg hasn't influenced you to change your mind?"

She nodded. Not directly, anyway. But how could she explain that she'd begun to see him in another light, not just as a money-hungry landowner trying to take advantage of his tenants? She admired the quiet wisdom he exuded. And any man who had made love to her as tenderly as he had... Well, in a word, she trusted him. Incredible, but true. "Greg and I haven't talked about the project since—for a while. In fact, the couple of times I tried to bring it up, he changed the subject. He has no idea I'm leaning in favor of his proposal."

"So have you told the other shop owners?"

She nodded. "We met twice this week to talk about the state of the neighborhood, which is rapidly declining. The truth is, I don't know if Greg's plan will work, but like it or not, his is the only plan that's being funded. If the shop owners negotiate a delay or a compromise, I'm afraid we're simply postponing the inevitable."

"So just like that, you're going to give in?"

"Alex, I know when to surrender."

"Then is now a good time to tell you that I agree with your new stance completely?"

Lana gaped. "But all along you've been saying—"

"That I would be there for moral support. Personally, I think Greg Healey is the best chance the Hyde Parkland area has to survive."

She put a hand to her temple. "But you enlisted Ms. Wheeler's help for the shop owners."

Alex nodded. "She and I both believe that even the best

ideas need to be challenged in case something better evolves."

Lana swallowed. "So you think Greg's plan is best."

"I'd prefer that some of the retail landscape be left intact, but the residential zoning is badly needed."

Jack was headed their way, looking as if he wanted to talk to his wife about something. Alex's hand was warm when she gave Lana's arm an affectionate squeeze. "We'll talk about this more later, okay?"

Lana nodded, feeling powerless. Her best friend, the council president, Greg—they'd all been humoring her? Pretending to consider her concerns when the decision had already been made? Her skin tingled with embarrassment and hurt. She realized Greg had no intention of their picking up where they'd left off after the rezoning project was decided. The rezoning project had *already* been decided.

Across the room, Greg was talking to a sleek redhead, an employee of Alex's who tossed her hair to effect. The cat-and-mouse game that Lana and Greg had been playing since she'd arrived had seemed playful and proprietary at first, but now seemed immature and manipulative. She took a deep drink of cranberry juice and grenadine, pursing her mouth and swallowing tightly. She glanced over again at Greg and the redhead—it looked like the cat had found the catnip.

"Lana!"

She conjured up a smile at the sound of Will's happy voice. He and Annette walked toward her, Annette clinging to his arm possessively. They looked adorable. "Hi, you two. Having a good time?" If nothing else good came out of this fiasco, at least *they* had found each other—a small miracle, really.

Will nodded and Annette squealed. "Isn't this a gorgeous house?"

"Absolutely," she agreed, taking another drink.

"Why aren't you with Gregory?" Will asked with a little frown.

Her pride smarting, Lana pointed. "Gregory is occupied."

The couple turned to look at Greg and the she-cat.

Will's frown deepened. "But he's supposed to be nice to *you*, Lana. We talked about it."

She frowned. Greg had talked to Will about their relationship? "What do you mean, Will?"

The big man was agitated now. "Gregory said he was going to be nice to you to win you over. Now he's messing things up."

A tiny alarm sounded in the back of her mind, but Lana laid a hand on his arm. "Calm down, Will. What do you mean 'win me over'?"

But Will looked confused, his eyes wide and troubled. Greg must have noticed Will's body language because he broke away from the woman and moved in their direction, his face a mask of concern. "Is something wrong, Will?"

"You're not being nice to Lana," he accused loudly.

From the shocked looked on Greg's face, she gathered Will rarely raised his voice.

"What are you talking about?" Greg asked, clearly puzzled.

Will shook his finger. "Shame on you, Gregory. You said you were going to be nice to Lana to win her over to your side—"

Her heart shivered and shrunk. She took one, two steps backward.

"—but you're over there being nice to someone else. Are you shutting down that other lady's business, too?"

The expression on Greg's face when his gaze met hers

could have best been described as guilt, pure and unadulterated guilt.

The picture was suddenly so clear. He'd slept with her to neutralize her opposition to the project. The outcome had already been decided, but he must have wanted to be certain she wouldn't pose a problem. Or maybe he saw the conquest as a bonus. Through the metallic hum in her ears, Lana heard a *thump* and felt moisture on her leg. She looked down and stared at the growing stain of cranberry juice on the expensive handwoven sisal. Alex would kill her for ruining her brand-new carpet.

In the midst of the small commotion that ensued, Lana slipped through the crowd toward the door. She didn't look back.

24

"MESSAGE ONE...Lana, it's Alex. Why did you leave in such a hurry last night? Call me."

"Message two...Lana, it's Greg. I need to explain about the things Will said last night. Call me."

"Message three...Lana, it's Mother. I'm back from the cruise. Call me so I can tell you all about it, dear."

"Message four...Lana, it's Greg. I went by the shop today thinking I'd find you there, but saw you were closed for New Year's. Please call me when you get this message."

"Message five...Lana, it's Alex. I went by the shop today thinking you might be open, then swung by your apartment, but you must have been out. I wanted to let you know that Buckhead Coffee has decided against renting space in Tremont's. And I want to find out how you're doing. Call me when you get in."

Lana set down her blue helmet, ruffled her hair and pushed a button to delete all the messages.

"Where have you been all day?" Rich asked, strolling into the living room.

"Oh, just riding around, looking for a new location for the coffee shop."

"Find anything?"

She shook her head. It had seemed like a good idea, but her heart wasn't in it—like looking for a new home when you truly loved the one you were already living in.

"Your phone has been ringing off the hook," he said.

"Sorry we got separated last night at the party. I didn't even realize you'd left."

"I should have told you. Did you have a good time?"

The smile on his face was answer enough, but he nodded. "I met some interesting people. Did you and Greg cut out early?"

"No," she said with a shaky smile. "Just me. I spilled my drink all over myself, and decided to leave before the night got any worse."

He angled his head at her. "Lovers' quarrel?"

"We're not lovers," she amended, then shrugged nonchalantly. "He was only being nice to me to win me over to his side of the rezoning project." She couldn't even say his name.

Rich made a rueful sound with his cheek. "How do you know that?"

"His brother told me."

"Is his brother trustworthy?"

"The man couldn't tell a lie if he wanted to."

"So you were under the impression that Greg was looking for a relationship when you slept with him?"

Lana shucked off her black-and-white spotted coat and hung it on Harry's obliging shoulder. "No. But I thought...I mean, I was hoping..."

"That he would fall in love with you and change his mind?" he asked softly.

She bit into her lip and blinked back hot tears. "Ridiculous, isn't it?"

"Not really. Like I said, you want to believe that people have good motivations. It's kind of refreshing."

Lana walked to the kitchen and filled her teakettle with water. "But it hurts," she murmured.

"So, you love this guy?"

She studied the water rushing into the kettle. Making tea

was such a soothing process. "I think I must, or else I wouldn't feel so lousy." Her laugh was humorless. "I've been alone most of my life and liked it that way. But now..."

"Everything's different?" He sat on a stool and leaned in to the counter. "When do you see him again?"

"Tomorrow morning we're meeting with the president of the city council to talk about the rezoning proposal for the last time before the council takes a vote."

"Sounds tense."

She shook her head. "I'm tired, Rich. I don't have the money, or the influence, or the energy. It's easier just to give people who have money what they want and get out of the way. I'd have been better off if I'd never fought Greg Healey. He's going to win, anyway, and all I'll have to show for it is a bankrupt business and a broken heart."

He cracked a tiny smile. "There's a country-western song in there somewhere."

She smiled in spite of herself, grateful that Rich had come into her life. "Will you watch the water while I change?" But her feet dragged during the short walk to her bedroom. She kept reliving the scene last night at the party, the look on Greg's face. She felt so...foolish. She'd been falling in love with the man, and he'd probably been laughing at her the entire time. Her face burned when she thought of her research and the notebook of ideas that he'd probably found laughably simplistic.

She'd obviously set her life goals too high—a good relationship with her parents, her own business...Greg. Time to regroup. Tomorrow she would find out how long she'd have to transfer out of business, and would start hitting the Help Wanted ads.

A wry frown curved her mouth. Back to the classifieds, where this whole miserable mess had started.

"ARE YOU MAD AT ME, Gregory?"

Greg lifted his eye from his telescope. He'd hoped to catch a glimpse of Lana today—maybe smiling or giving some indication that she didn't hate him as much as he thought she did—but he'd given up and turned his attention to Orion, the Hunter, featuring the red star of Betelgeuse. He sighed at the anguished look on his brother's face. "Of course I'm not mad at you."

"Annette said I stuck my foot in your mouth."

"I'm starting to like Annette," Greg murmured.

"Did I ruin things between you and Lana?"

"Nope," Greg said, dropping into an overstuffed chair. "I did that all by myself."

"Don't you like Lana?"

He pressed his lips together, then nodded. "Yeah, I like her a lot."

"Do you love her?"

Greg swung his head around in surprise. "I, uh...it doesn't matter. She doesn't feel that way about me."

"How do you know?"

"How could she, after what I'm about to do?"

"Close her shop?"

He nodded.

"But do you have to close her shop?"

"We've been through this, Will, and the money—"

"Isn't Lana more important than money?"

Greg blinked. Will had never interrupted him before. *Never.* "I—"

"Gregory, I'm not always going to be around to take care of you, you know."

Greg's eyebrows lifted.

"So if you love Lana, you'd better find a way to get her to love you back."

Greg felt his jaw loosen. Will was giving *him* relationship advice?

"And as far as the business goes," Will continued, "Daddy left me half, didn't he?"

Incredulity gripped him. Will had never shown an ounce of interest in the company. Was he threatening to *veto* Greg's decision?

"Look into your heart, Gregory, and do the right thing."

"LET'S TRY TO KEEP this brief," councilwoman Wheeler said with a smile as she closed her office door. "A few weeks ago I charged the two of you to come up with a compromise on the Hyde Parkland revitalization project—a plan that would please the landowner and the existing merchants. Were you able to reach a compromise?"

"No," Lana said without looking in Greg's direction. Her skin tingled at his proximity. She had a death grip on the bag that held his repaired jacket, which she intended to throw in his face at an appropriate time. Hopefully soon. She wanted to get this over with, quickly. "But the merchants—"

"Yes," Greg cut in. "I'll be presenting a compromise to the city council next week which I think will please all parties."

Lana swung her head to narrow her eyes at him. "Is this another trick?" she murmured, breaking her vow not to speak to him.

"No. Just hear me out."

"We're listening, Mr. Healey."

He opened his briefcase and withdrew a foldout poster. "These drawings are a little crude, but basically the modified proposal details the development of a village in the Hyde Parkland area."

"A village?" Lana parroted.

He nodded. "Structures that would house a store on the first floor, and living quarters for the business owner above."

"Like an old-time village," Wheeler said, obviously warming to the idea.

"Exactly," Greg said, nodding enthusiastically. "If two blocks of Hyde Parkland were developed in this fashion, then most of the retail landscape could be retained, and more businesses would be attracted. Food shops, hair salons, service businesses—we would cater to the small business owner who wants the convenience of being close to his or her shop. When everything is renovated, it'll be the best of the old and the new—sidewalks, parks, lampposts, awnings."

Lana could only gape.

The councilwoman hummed her approval. "Well done, Mr. Healey, Ms. Martina. Much better than leveling blocks and starting over. I knew you could come up with something if the two of you worked together. I assume you have a developer who's interested in executing the plan?"

"The primary developer pulled out when I presented this idea, but I have two smaller companies who are interested. The time line will be longer than we previously discussed—maybe as long as three years."

"What's three years?" Wheeler asked. "We're talking about the future of downtown Lexington."

"My feelings exactly," Greg said.

Lana's head was spinning. She certainly couldn't deny the attractiveness of the idea—a village atmosphere would be the perfect solution for the neighborhood. But why the sudden change of heart?

She met his gaze, knowing her confusion was clear. He stared back, his eyes shining with what seemed like regret, or guilt.

There was a knock on the door, and someone who needed to speak with the councilwoman appeared. "I'll be right back," Ms. Wheeler promised, then left them in an awkward silence.

Lana squirmed on the hard chair, afraid to look at him, afraid to get drawn in again by what she wanted to see.

"I'm sorry about the other night," Greg said softly. "I can imagine what you must think of me."

"Good," she said. "Then I don't have to tell you."

"I want to see you again."

Her breath froze in her chest. A blip of happiness at his request was overridden by the memory of the past couple of days. Greg was too easy to love, and he'd never feel the same way about her. "No," she said, shaking her head. "We're too different, Greg, and—"

"I love you."

She gripped the edges of the chair to steady herself, and her pulse. "What?" she croaked.

"I love you. I want us to be together."

Lana stood abruptly, making a chopping motion with her hand. "I'm not having this conversation." She blinked furious tears. "You get me down here, knowing I'm expecting the worst, then spring this idea on me, which is pretty good, but you could have had the decency to share it earlier, and now you've decided that you love me and that we should be together, and you think you can just snap your fingers, and I'll come running?"

A little frown marred his brow. "Is that a question?"

"I'm out of here."

"Lana—"

"Don't," she said, raising her hand like a crossing guard. Her tears were falling freely now. "You've put me through a lot the past few weeks. Excuse me if I don't want to be manipulated anymore." Remembering the jacket, she flung it at him, then walked to the door, wiping her eyes. "Give my apologies to Ms. Wheeler."

LANA LAY on the beanbag chair, looking up at the ceiling, enjoying the floating sensation. She hadn't been able to go back to the shop after the meeting, so she'd called Alex and apologized for ruining the rug, which led to a crying jag, then had spent the afternoon in the beanbag, replaying what Greg had said during the meeting. *I love you. I want us to be together. I love you. I want us to be together. I love you. I want us to be together.*

Together, how? Together, dating? Together, live together? Together, married?

"What am I going to do, Harry?" she asked her sidekick, who was dressed again in his striped pajamas. "The man scares me. I've known him for a few weeks, and he completely wrecked my life."

Harry grinned.

"I was willing to let him bulldoze my coffee shop because I trusted him so much to do what was right."

Harry grinned.

"Do you think if he were in a similar situation, he'd be willing to make such a big sacrifice for me?"

Harry grinned.

"But if I give up now, I'll never know."

Harry grinned.

"You're right!" she cried, and grabbed the doll to give him a smooch on the cheek. Then she picked up the phone with a shaky hand. She'd dialed three numbers when she glanced toward the balcony and an idea took root. With a sudden burst of energy, she slammed down the phone and went to the bedroom for supplies.

GREG DROPPED onto the foot of his bed to remove his shoes. What a day. What a disconcerting, chaotic day. The meeting with Wheeler, the phone call to turn down the job offer, the hours-long staff meeting to outline the new, more relaxed, company policies.

It had been a big decision to give up the chance at criminal law, but Greg had taken Will's words to heart. Not only was Lana more important to him than money, but she meant more to him than a job in the courthouse.

But the satisfaction of making decisions and setting the wheels in motion was tempered by his disappointment over Lana's reaction to his proclamation. He was a proud man. Words like *I love you* did not spill out of his mouth easily. Call him vain, but he'd expected a better response.

He closed his eyes. Complicated. He'd fallen in love with a complicated woman. He didn't know how, but he was going to wear her down. He was going to, as Will said, find a way to get her to love him back.

Will. He laughed. What a surprise his brother could be.

Greg pushed himself to his tired feet, peeled off his shirt, then splashed his face with cold water. Moving slowly— damn, he was feeling old—he spun the telescope around, pointing it northwest in the falling dusk, hoping for a good view of Cassiopeia, the Queen. The constellation was dim but visible, and promised a brighter show later in the month. Whistling tunelessly, he spun the telescope toward the skyline, more out of habit than out of hope. When he focused on her apartment building, he lifted his head, squinted, then looked again. Something was draped across her balcony. A sheet. A sheet with lettering.

He adjusted the power of the lens, then refocused. Yes, it was a sheet with...a message. His heart beat faster as he linked the large, black letters into words. He read them out loud. "'Complicated...woman...seeking...single...male.'"

Greg's heart vaulted in his chest.

_____Epilogue_____

"WHAT ARE YOU going to do with Harry?" Greg asked, draping his arm around the grinning doll's shoulders.

Lana straightened from packing a box and smiled. "Alex is getting me the address of the Valentine sisters. We knew them in college, and Alex thinks they're both still single. One of them will be the lucky recipient of Harry."

Greg scratched his head. "What happens when everyone is eventually married?"

She frowned. "Well, if statistics bear out, someone's bound to be single again sometime."

He walked over and gathered her in his arms. "Not you, Mrs. Healey."

She laughed. "*Lana Healey*. It still sounds so strange."

"But good," he murmured, nuzzling her cheek. "Will and I had a discussion about that very thing right after he met you." He laughed. "Of course, at the time he thought *he* would marry you."

"I can't imagine him with anyone but Annette."

"And I can't imagine me with anyone but you."

A little thrill raced through her at the sight of the love in his dark eyes. Lately he looked years younger, his features more relaxed, his mouth more apt to smile. Lana sighed. "I love our life. You, husband, were brilliant on TV last night. Alex says your company is bound to win all kinds of awards for engineering such an innovative revitalization plan."

"We still have a long way to go."

"You're off to an impressive start." She angled her head

at him. "You're so...persuasive when you want to be. You would've made a great criminal lawyer."

A tiny smile softened his mouth.

"Did you ever think about it?"

"Oh, once or twice," he said, then shrugged. "But it just wasn't my cuppa...Joe."

He pulled her into his embrace and she buried her nose in his soft sweatshirt. Holy happily-ever-after. Here was the male she'd been seeking all along.

* * * * *

Travel with Harry the blow-up doll to Chicago,
where he'll take up residence with a woman
whose opposition to marriage makes her a dynamite
challenge to Harry's matchmaking aura!

When spurned-at-the-altar Rebecca Valentine turns the
Closed sign on the costume shop she owns, she escapes
into a fantasy world she's created in the dressing room in
the back of her store. Central to her fantasies—her best
customer, Michael Pierce. The fact that he's married
makes him safely off-limits to her healing heart.

Michael Pierce owns Incognito, a popular Chicago
restaurant that features waiters and waitresses in
costume. Having just ended a disastrous marriage, he has
little interest in romance—until he accidentally witnesses
demure little Rebecca Valentine in a dress-up
(and down) performance!

Look for Stephanie Bond's next sizzling story in a
Harlequin Blaze Anthology entitled
MIDNIGHT FANTASIES,
mid-2001.

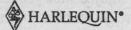

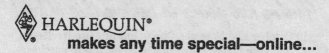

You're not going to believe this offer!

In October and November 2000, buy any two Harlequin or Silhouette books and save $10.00 off future purchases, or buy any three and save $20.00 off future purchases!

Just fill out this form and attach 2 proofs of purchase (cash register receipts) from October and November 2000 books and Harlequin will send you a coupon booklet worth a total savings of $10.00 off future purchases of Harlequin and Silhouette books in 2001. Send us 3 proofs of purchase and we will send you a coupon booklet worth a total savings of $20.00 off future purchases.

Saving money has never been this easy.

I accept your offer! Please send me a coupon booklet:

Name: _____

Address: _____ City: _____

State/Prov.: _____ Zip/Postal Code: _____

Optional Survey!

In a typical month, how many Harlequin or Silhouette books would you buy <u>new</u> at retail stores?

☐ Less than 1   ☐ 1   ☐ 2   ☐ 3 to 4   ☐ 5+

Which of the following statements best describes how you <u>buy</u> Harlequin or Silhouette books? Choose one answer only that <u>best</u> describes you.

☐ I am a regular buyer and reader
☐ I am a regular reader but buy only occasionally
☐ I only buy and read for specific times of the year, e.g. vacations
☐ I subscribe through Reader Service but also buy at retail stores
☐ I mainly borrow and buy only occasionally
☐ I am an occasional buyer and reader

Which of the following statements best describes how you <u>choose</u> the Harlequin and Silhouette series books you buy <u>new</u> at retail stores? By "series," we mean books within a particular line, such as *Harlequin PRESENTS* or *Silhouette SPECIAL EDITION.* Choose one answer only that <u>best</u> describes you.

☐ I only buy books from my favorite series
☐ I generally buy books from my favorite series but also buy books from other series on occasion
☐ I buy some books from my favorite series but also buy from many other series regularly
☐ I buy all types of books depending on my mood and what I find interesting and have no favorite series

Please send this form, along with your cash register receipts as proofs of purchase, to:
In the U.S.: Harlequin Books, P.O. Box 9057, Buffalo, NY 14269
In Canada: Harlequin Books, P.O. Box 622, Fort Erie, Ontario L2A 5X3
(Allow 4-6 weeks for delivery) Offer expires December 31, 2000.   PHQ4002

It's hot...and it's out of control.

This winter is going to be hot, hot, hot!
Don't miss these bold, provocative,
ultra-sexy books!

SEDUCED by Janelle Denison
December 2000

Lawyer Ryan Matthews wanted sexy Jessica Newman the
moment he saw her. And she seemed to want him, too, but
something was holding her back. So Ryan decides it's time
to launch a sensual assault. He *is* going to have Jessica in
his bed—and he isn't above tempting her with her own
forbidden fantasies to do it....

SIMPLY SENSUAL by Carly Phillips
January 2001

When P.I. Ben Callahan agrees to take the job of watching
over spoiled heiress Grace Montgomery, he figures it's easy
money. That is, until he discovers gorgeous Grace has a
reckless streak a mile wide and is a serious threat to his
libido—and his heart. Ben isn't worried about keeping
Grace safe. But can he protect her from his loving lies?

Don't miss this daring duo!